A Wa

by

Acknowledgements:

(So many more than this.)

My Dad, for being my editor among other things.

My sister Rebecca, for that excellent brainstorming session way too early at Tim Hortons.

My brother Johnathon, who pushed me to finish it so he could read it.

My wonderful Mother, who read the book with her ingenious eye.

My godsis, Jennifer Williams, who listened to me ramble about my stories while trying to write her own.

My Discord buddy and customer Merlin – sorry about your character, buddy. Congrats on the baby, though!

My Grandma and Grandpa Dady, who didn't let me stay up too late writing.

Chapter 1

The laughter of the children rang out in the late afternoon. Peals of giggles scattered themselves through the encampment of the Red Elf tribe. The women of the tribe watched the children, rolling their eyes, chuckling to themselves and engaged in idle chatter while going about their usual duties. The sun with its pillows of clouds slowly making their way to it was setting over the idyllic scene of tents, water-barrels, hunting-drakes, and horses. Both mounts were in their own circular pens, on opposite sides of the camp towards the front.

To the right and about fifty yards away from the scene of youthful joy and more mature business, there was a group of mature oak trees that seemed to have eschewed themselves from Trepidation Forest, the forest parallel to the encampment of the Reds, about 100 acres from it.

From high in one of those trees – an old, fair one with branches perfect for climbing – a figure watched. His green cloak was around his shoulders and pulled tightly around him, hood up over his head. His breathing was silent, echoing his many years of training.

He was there as the enemy.

Not that he wanted to be categorized as such, but he was proclaimed the enemy by the Red tribe, for he was a Green elf. His name was Aldrin, last of the Green elves, save those on the Council of Four, and he was watching the women and children of the tribe that brutally wiped out his tribe.

Women and children... He kept mulling the words in his mind. *They are not my enemy,* he thought, quietly taking his bow off of his shoulders.

But they are the wives and children of your enemy, Aldrin, retorted another thought. *Why should you care about their protection?* He grimaced slightly as he remembered those words, spoken by his superior officer.

He concentrated as he reached over his shoulder to the quiver of arrows at his back and pulled an arrow from it. He had been fortunate – or unfortunate – enough to be close to a Purple encampment and had overheard in their language of guttural snarls and clicks that they were going to attack an encampment – *this* encampment. He was still debating his seething dislike for the Red Tribe, but everyone had every right to hate the Purples. Especially since they said, as well as he could make out, they would "relieve the males of their chief distractions." Then they burst into terrifying laughter.

And I don't think they mean they're going to ban the trench-game Delie, he thought and his lips tugged into a grim smile, despite himself. His humor had not entirely deserted him.

Aldrin heard footsteps of the elven soldiers and their mounts as the Red tribe's men came back from the afternoon's hunt. He watched half the men trail off to the side to the circle of hunting drakes to dismount, while the rest crossed through the first guarding ring of the tents. The Green heard shouts of welcome and joy from youngling voices and women. He had to smile and he sighed. He remembered those times; times when he would come back to the encampment and find his legs bound by the embrace of his two little ones, his young daughter and younger son. His wife would come out of the tent behind them, her smile bright in the moonlight…

Oh, Malendire…

He had to stop. A tear flowed down his face and dribbled onto his knee. There were no little ones now. There was no wife now.

He looked at the sun as it was slowly being enveloped in dark clouds. He had been up in this tree for over four hours, watching the small family encampment. He had watched for the men to come back, wishing they would come more quickly than the daily hunt called for.

A Warrior's Code

Tonight would be a quick battle, and he did not think the Reds would win. The Purples were the fiercest warrior elf race Aldrin had ever seen. They were legendary; wild and savage. Sometimes they would group together as a unit, and that was when they were the most deadly. And what's more…

A shadow pressed against the back of his mind and his ears twitched behind him. He followed with his eyes, not to where the Red men had come from but slightly angled to the left of it.

He saw a massive dust storm black and thunderous, coming from the forest and he squinted at it, trying to clear his head. This was the major way the Purple Elves caught their prey: paralyzing through gripping fear. Like the paralyzing gaze of a cobra against a sparrow. But he was far enough away to shake the effects of the mental imagery and he finally perceived through the trees a group of ten, maybe twenty Purples.

Unlike the other elves who shared the same skin color save for the odd foreigner from the Southern or Eastern territories, the Purples were literally purple. And they were gorilla-like and massive with fanged jaws and perilous eyes that seemed to glow. Twenty was enough if not too much for a single encampment, even for the Reds. He had heard rumors of just four taking down a small herd of buffalo.

Aldrin slunk down the tree into a nearby bush, using an old ingrained technique of the mind to mask his approach. He could not save them all, but he wanted to save at least *one*, if not two. He scampered quietly down the hill into the valley as at the same time the Purples entered the encampment, their determined walk becoming savage gallops. They burst through the first line of tents and Aldrin saw a middle-aged male get tackled. It was too late for him. However, his cry or the sense of the Purples had alerted the rest of the encampment and two more elves had darted off to release the hunting drakes. *Would it be too late for all of them?* Aldrin wondered.

He could hear the screams of the women and children intermingled with the warrior cries of the men, Red and Purple alike. He swiftly dashed to one of the tents, diving behind a barrel of water as one of the wingless dragons thundered past him, missing him by inches. He looked up just in time to see the tent open and a lady elf run out.

She was pregnant. "Dairlo!" she cried to her husband in the tent. Lit up by the small lantern and perhaps a fire set in the tent, Aldrin could see the silhouette of the male elf was overshadowed by a bigger shadow he was fiercely grappling with.

"I'll be fine, Zachtia," called her mate, "Just go! Go to the city!"

Aldrin reached into his quiver and got his bow ready as she fled. He heard a Purple give a shout and he ducked as two ran past him after the female. He quickly aimed his arrow and fired, the arrow finding a place in the closest Purple's calf. With a fierce cry, the Purple fell.

He then sprinted after the other Purple. There was a forest about 100 yards from the encampment and the lady darted into it with the Purple hot on her trail. Aldrin pursued the two straight into the forest, casting aside the stories of what happens there at night.

His ears picked up no more running, only random scuttling. He slowed his pace and looked around – the tree branches were too high for him to climb up. He could jump, but he would risk being heard.

What to do…in this pitch he virtually could not see anything. He would have to go by hearing…as well as that pressing feeling of fear, which he pressed back against, physically setting his jaw tightly and slowing his breathing. This fear was an apparition – it was unreal, the feeling of a pressing fog or cloud just enhancing the beastly reality.

He considered his other options. Fortunately, the Purple was at an equal loss; he was going in the dark as well, though Aldrin didn't know to what extent the Purples could adapt to the dark.

He heard the sound of a heavy heartbeat, getting slowly louder. He tried to keep calm and repeated his thoughts about his quarry. *Savage, beast-like, ran on instinct…* and it occurred to him then exactly how to defeat it.

He quickly put his arrow away. He remembered the stories about how people got lost in the woods usually in the summer time…when it was hot and muggy. The Green's intelligence had found that it was due to Ender, a vine with an aromatic excretion that made an elf's senses go haywire, not to mention gave him a *major* migraine.

Aldrin searched around, feeling about with his hands and his feet until he reached a tree that had vines growing on it. After a test smell and having his eyes cross immediately afterward, he took his dagger and cut the Ender down and into manageable pieces.

He could hear his quarry – he guessed the heavy footfalls were his quarry – and got his Sparkstone ready. He mentally braced himself for the same pain he was about to give the Purple.

Sure enough, the Purple burst out of the brush about five feet to the left of him. He struck the Sparkstone with his knife and true to its name, the sparks hit the Ender and the extremely flammable weed burst into flame.

The smell of the burning Ender attacked and overpowered Aldrin and the Purple's senses. He saw through watering eyes and vertigo that the Purple was covering his eyes and nose, stumbling this way and that, screaming in a voice that made Aldrin's skin crawl.

Aldrin could barely keep himself up as he staggered away. He squinted through his kaleidoscoping vision, fighting the urge to throw up.

He fumbled as fast as he could through the forest and found a tree that he thought could support his weight, at least for the time being. The first time he tried to climb up it his head swam and he fell off feet first. He tried a second time with better results, climbing to the third branch and clung to the trunk of the tree to keep from falling. In a few moments, to his relief, he felt the pitter-patter of rain starting to fall…and in a few seconds it was a downpour – he would not have to go back to douse the fire.

Slowly, the smell relinquished its grip on his senses and he started tracing the steps of the Red, his eyes now a little more adjusted to the lighting. Aldrin put his hood over his head, making a mental note to change the color of it. *Perhaps a dark aqua?* he mused. He could not decide at the moment, but for right now, as a Green, he stuck out like a sore thumb.

He had been looking for around half an hour when his ears again picked up a heartbeat. It was strong and beating very quickly, even more quickly when he took a step to his ri –

Suddenly a rock flew from the direction he was looking and clipped the tip of his ear. Another one was soon following, and he dodged it. A third one! …this one he caught. "Are you the Red that I saw being chased by two Purples?" he called out.

The heart beat even faster, but no voice was heard. Aldrin sighed and tried again. "I overheard that the Purples were going to destroy your encampment. I wanted to do something…but I know that we are on different sides."

Again silence…but the heartbeat was just a little slower.

Aldrin squinted at where the rocks had been hurtled and realized that the large, dark blob he was looking at in front of him was actually an outcropping in a side of a hill. "I...don't want to hurt you."

"That's a laugh," came the Red's voice. "My husband told me about you Greens."

Stunned – though, not totally surprised – about this response, Aldrin said, "Alright, what did he tell you?"

Another rock came and he simply batted it away with a grunt. The Red's voice came again, "Enough to know that you'll kill me first chance you get. You Greens think you are so clever, don't you?"

"...not clever enough to best you Reds," replied Aldrin. "I'm the last, except for the four on the Council."

"Ha! You're quite the comic, you know that?" scoffed the Red. "One cannot simply wipe out an entire race of elves."

"The Reds did!" called Aldrin, struggling to keep his voice calm. "They slaughtered my people, every single Green elf they could find – I have been searching for *years*! No other Greens are alive."

The Red was silent.

Aldrin stood there, soaking in the rain and weighing his options. He could just leave. She was a Red, she could fend for herself. It would be easy.

... who was he trying to fool? *No, it wouldn't be easy*, he thought a moment later. *The women and children are not my enemy.* If he were to leave her now, he'd have more guilt stacked onto his soul. The Purple – possibly both or just the one he hadn't injured – could still be out there. For at least his sake, let alone hers, he would have to see this through.

He went to one knee in front of the outcropping. He held up his right hand as his left took the knife off of his belt, noticing

Zachtia's heartbeat quickening again. He extended the hand, the pommel of the knife loosely gripped with the knife edge pointing down. "I promise that no harm will come to you. I give you my word.

"A Green's word?" the Red's voice finally came from the blackness, edgy and unsure. "…How much worth is that to a Red?"

"As much as her life is to her, I assure you…" Aldrin let the knife fall from his hands, blade into the ground, signifying to her it was her decision that chose where he would go.

Finally, she said resolutely, "Alright…I'll trust you…but understand for only tonight…*only* because I'm tired and I'd rather die by the hands of a Green than a *Purple*. You are still my enemy *and be ready* to be treated as such tomorrow."

He took a few steps closer, unfastened his cloak, rolled it up into a makeshift pillow, and handed it to her. "I am afraid it is a bit damp," he said sympathetically.

Zachtia did not offer a smile, but she took the cloak and positioned it under her head.

Aldrin turned around to watch the forest, and heard the cloak slosh as she lay down on her back. "…I have a headache, anyway," he heard her say and turned to ask her if she was acquiring a better disposition, but she had fallen asleep at once.

He turned back to the night and got his bow and an arrow ready.

This was going to be a long night.

Chapter 2

Zachtia slept through the rest of the night and some of the next morning. When she awoke, Aldrin had already gone out and caught two rabbits; one rabbit's pelt was on the forest floor and its bones were scattered on it, the other rabbit was stripped of its skin and on a makeshift spit which the elf was turning slowly.

She propped herself up and looked at his clothing. He was a Green elf, sure enough. His hat that was shaped like the beak of an eagle – it was green. His semi-form-fitting shirt and multi-pocketed pants were green, too. She looked at the cloak her head had been on – it was green. The only things that were not green on the elf were a pair of brown, hart-skin boots.

He turned to her. "Good morning," he said.

"The same to you, Green," she said warily, sitting most of the way up. Morning sickness was not too prevalent this morning and she was going to take advantage of that. She took her "pillow" up in her hands and tossed it to the Green elf and he caught it easily.

"You're welcome," he said and she gave a curt nod.

The Green turned the spit one more time, took the skewered rabbit off of the spit and put it on a large, damp stone. "I was keeping it warm for you," he said, referring to the rabbit. "I was going to catch some fish but that would have taken too long." He proffered his knife to her. "You trusted me not to kill you…can I do the same?"

She took it from his hands slowly and cut into the rabbit meat. "My hand was a bit forced, don't you think?" She stabbed the small square of meat and took a sniff…smelled okay.

"If there was going to be poison, it would have been from the malanda leaf," said Aldrin quietly. "Kills instantly and exits the body through the pores. However, malanda poison is rendered harmless when put to a flame. That's why when you brush up against a malanda plant you should temporarily light that skin on fire therefore dissipating the –"

Zachtia pointed the knife at him. "Are you going to be quiet anytime soon?"

Aldrin put his hands up. "I apologize if my talking is making you uncomfortable," he began cautiously.

"It's not the talking – it's the 'not stopping' that is making me uncomfortable." She pointed at her breakfast. "Can I eat in peace?"

"Alright." Aldrin sat quietly and let her finish her meal without uttering a word. Zachtia found it almost amusing, watching this grown elf fidgeting and looking uncomfortable as she ate. After she was finished, she was handed a cloth to clean her hands and face. She took it without a word and after wiping her mouth she said, "So, what now, Green? If you're not going to kill me, what do you plan on doing with me?"

She watched as the Green chose his words carefully. "Well…" he said, "that is your choice, Zachtia…but I would like for you to consider a few things." He began numbering the "few things" on his fingers: "You are heading to a city with a baby in your womb with only the knowledge on how to get there, no other Reds around, Purples like to roam free in this day and age, and wild beasts *besides* the Purples like to roam around and have a taste for our blood." He pointed to himself. "I am the last of my tribe, in my mid-hundreds, fully knowledgeable on the herbs that can kill you and those that won't…and I have already expressed and semi-proven that I don't want to hurt you and, on the contrary, I want to help you." He looked straight into her eyes. "…I put it before you again. What do you want to do?"

She looked at him…

…and stood up. "Have you stay in the front."

As faithful as Zachtia's late draglet Samys, Aldrin stayed in front of Zachtia. Watching him from behind gave the Red a puzzling revelation: he actually wanted to look out for her. There could not be any doubt, really; the way his head darted around, how his bow and arrow were always at hand. He periodically called out for directions and updates on how she was.

Deep down, she was relieved, actually. Having a person – even a *Green* – looking after her gave her at least a little piece of mind.

During the third hour of the trek through the woods, they both froze at a noise – a very gravelly, staunch rumbling that sounded like it was coming from a very large creature.

Aldrin already had his arrow ready. "Get ready to dart, Zachtia. Don't run – that'll attract its attention."

"What's '*it*'?" asked Zachtia in a panicked fury.

"From the sound, it's likely a female doepine," Aldrin said, tracking another rumble emitted to the right of them, "Tall legs, claws, teeth, and a snake-like prehensile tail. It's good for meat, though."

"That's probably what it's thinking about *us*, Green," cried Zachtia.

Suddenly Aldrin whipped his bow to his right. "*Down!*" he shouted as he let loose an arrow.

Zachtia had no argument there. She ducked as the spindly doepine darted into the clearing they were in and at the same time Aldrin had let loose his arrow. It struck its target, but only in the upper thigh of its right leg. Snarling and making that horrific rumbling noise that seemed to vibrate every nerve in Zachtia's body, the creature made another pass at Aldrin, swiping at him with its claws.

Aldrin dodged these easily, catching up his knife from his belt and taking a swing at the creature. This time he missed and the creature staggered back to a safe distance, snarling and showing a row of vicious fangs. Its eyes locked onto Zachtia and it was all Zachtia could do not to scream as it charged her!

…but it never got to her. Aldrin launched himself as well, slamming into the creature with full force. His head rammed into its neck, the doepine's teeth scratching his face. In midair, he took his opportunity and drove the business end of his knife into the creature's neck and yanked up through its jaw.

In a few seconds, Zachtia watched as Aldrin untangled himself from the bloody corpse of the doepine, breathing heavily. He looked at Zachtia, "You alright?" he asked.

When she nodded, a little faint, he looked back at the doepine. "…we shouldn't waste this meat…almost lunch time, anyway."

As he dug his knife back into the beast, this time to skin it, Zachtia felt her consciousness slip from her as she fainted…and was woken up by Aldrin lightly shaking her. "Zachtia, I'm done," he said.

She waved him off and looked at what was before her. He had not only skinned the animal, but he had also set up a fire site in the clearing and now was cooking the meat on a spit.

She slowly sat up, her body giving her protest and Aldrin handed her the same flat stone he had served her the rabbit on, this time with doepine meat on it. "Still hot," he said quietly.

When she took the meal and his knife, he went back to his fire.

Halfway through her meal, Zachtia said, "So tell me…what is your name?" She knew full well she was committing a wartime taboo, being friendly with the enemy. But he *had* just saved her from the doepine. So the truce between them was still in place.

"Aldrin," said Aldrin.

"…how did you become the sole survivor of our so-called 'greatest enemy'?" The Red took another bite of her portion.

Aldrin breathed out slowly. "I am one of the Bacht, Green Division."

Zachtia raised an eyebrow, surprised. "A Bacht? That's an elite fighting force division…I thought Greens were all academic!"

Aldrin shook his head. "That's a common misconception – it's the very reason why the Yellow tribe stuck to us like sap: they are the pure academic ones; they are too cowardly to fight, and so they have become the so-called 'invisible' tribe."

Zachtia stared at him with a blank face. "And what does that have to do with…?"

"I'm getting to that part. If I'm going to make clear a misconception that has multiple branches, I should clear up the branches, would you not agree?"

The Red sighed. "Typical Green."

"I could say the same about you," Aldrin replied softly. "Typical Red – always impatiently wanting the point and the end, no matter what means they skip."

She tried to detect some malice in his voice, but there was none as he continued,

"You and I are totally different and I'm not saying that just to state the obvious. If I am going to protect you until you get to the city that you're going to…then we have to get along and compromise. I'll try to talk more concisely if you'll slow down your listening, alright?"

Zachtia looked at his eyes…not just to acknowledge she was listening, but just to make a pure study of his eyes. They were a pure, pale blue that complimented his attire. Instead of the high or wary tone that she had been expecting from him, his tone of voice reminded her of her husband whenever he was telling her how he disagreed with what happened in battle or a general's orders. It was a very pure tone, like a bell ringing softly in her ear. She sighed again, but this time she made a decision. "Alright," she said to Aldrin, "…the 'invisible' tribe…?"

A grin flashed on his face as he continued, "We Greens had the ability and the patience to study information and, in most cases, apply it."

Zachtia listened and caught on, "…and the Yellows were the ones that got you your information."

"Exactly!" said Aldrin, "We developed our information into knowledge, knowledge into wisdom, and wisdom into a way of living. But we were not ignorant. We also developed strategies and weapons to use against our enemies, along with medical facts and the healing arts. The Yellows and the Greens made a pact: we would protect them and they would give us a feed of information." Aldrin leaned back. "I just summed up about 12 years of Green history for you – concise enough?"

She had to smile at that. "Knowing what I know now about you Greens, I can handle such…conciseness. But I have no idea why our tribes are such enemies, Aldrin. Explain that, please!"

Aldrin shrugged. "Your guess is as good as mine. My commander once said that there was a clash between Green and Red on the Council and that's what started it off and I tend to believe him."

She was quiet. "Concise," she said softly.

"You asked me to be," he replied tonelessly, but with a wry grin.

She had to consider again. She had determined she was going to be nice to him, but was she actually getting into a *joking* quarrel with this Green?

She finished her meal in thoughtful silence. "You know," she began afterwards, "I am part of an arrow-construction guild and we talk while we are working. It would be deathly boring if we didn't talk. We talk about the different tribes and your tribe brings up the most debate."

She left off there and the Green looked expectantly at her. "…debate," she continued, "that has led a few of us to wonder if our priorities are not skewered in some form or fashion."

"Indeed." Aldrin said. He sighed softly. "I think I'll have to get used to this…conciseness."

They both chuckled and looked away from each other. It was Aldrin who spoke first. "Zachtia," he said softly, "I know you're married…and I know you bear his child. I give you my word that I will protect you and this life inside you until we get to the city."

"Scarlesh," she said. She turned to him. "I need to go to Scarlesh."

"Scarlesh…" Aldrin seemed to be rolling the name around on his tongue as he stood up. His pointer finger danced and jittered as he muttered silently. "That's four days at regular soldier speed…"

"How about 'pregnant elf' speed?" asked Zachtia, standing up with his help.

"About a week," he replied.

"Hm," she grunted. "As to your earlier comment, thank you. I'm encouraged in your knowledge that I am a mate and the proof of my mateship is prevalent, also in the knowledge that I will be protected by you. My only question is, why are you telling me this?" She held up her index finger as he started and said with a slight smile, "Concisely."

He stared at her. His lips pursed and Zachtia could sense the cogs clunking in his brain as he strove to be less verbose. "Friendship," he said finally.

The Red elf cocked her head to the side. "Alright, I admit I asked for that – a little less concise…what about friendship?"

"I wish to be your protector and to do that to the extent needed I must become your friend. If I didn't make my intentions clear, there could be…tension between us."

Zachtia blinked.

Twice.

She then took in a deep breath and said, "To be fair, I thought as much – about being friends and all. In a way I must thank you again – you have released me of my duty of telling you I'm a married woman."

She let out a puff of air. "Alright, a friendship it is, then. You can talk about your wife and I will talk about my husband equally." She held out her forearm in compliance with Council regulations on agreements. "Deal?"

"In this case I – deal," he said. In equal accordance, he raised his own forearm and bumped it against hers.

A Warrior's Code

Chapter 3

They cleared the forest in about a day. In that time, they said very few words to each other, which Aldrin could understand…somewhat. He was feeling talkative, but he knew his Red companion was not in the mood.

They had to rest repeatedly, for Zachtia's sake. The baby inside her was about four months from being born, but, like with all elven children developing in the womb, it was already starting to kick.

Zachtia broke the silence before Aldrin could. When they cleared the trees and stepped through to a reasonably flat plane of ground she breathed in and said, "Finally! I thought we would become two of the lost."

Aldrin looked at her. "You have those stories, too? The lost of the Forest?"

"Oh yes, very much so."

The Red elf squinted into the distance. "About a mile off…we'll have to cross a river. From what I can tell, there are a lot of stones, but they look smooth in the ankle-deep water."

Aldrin squinted. "Thank you. Because of a preexisting condition, I don't have that kind of sight."

"Really?" Zachtia looked surprised. "How far can you make out?"

"Eh…" Aldrin willed his eyesight to shift to its full extent. "… to that lone tree right there," he finally said, pointing to a middle-aged tree that had a full complement of leaves.

"Well, that's not too much of a crisis," Zachtia replied reassuringly. "That's about half a mile you can see clearly."

She fell silent and he looked back at her, reeling his senses back in so she wasn't just a blob of fuzziness. She was staring at him, brows furrowed slightly. "You just told me a weakness, Aldrin."

Aldrin started. "Clumsy."

"Talkative, more likely."

"Well!" exclaimed the Green elf, "When you've not been able to talk to someone you trust in a while, things tend to slip out!"

A slight smile came onto Zachtia's face as she looked at him. "Someone you trust, Aldrin?"

"Yes…" Aldrin looked away. "I don't want to be the enemy."

"Ever considered just doing the ritual of becoming a Red?" the Red elf asked sincerely.

Aldrin nodded slowly. "I have thought about that," he said softly.

"And what did you conclude?"

"I concluded that I'd rather stay associated with the tribe that I was born into, raised with…married with." He took a deep breath and continued, "I have a Green's history and honor."

"Mm." She looked away from him. "A Green's honor…I think I can live with that until we get into Scarlesh."

"I'm confident your husband will be waiting for you," said Aldrin reassuringly.

The sentence hung in the air. For a moment Zachtia was quiet. Aldrin did not know what to do until he heard her say softly, "I surely hope so."

They continued forward, and true to Zachtia's word they came upon a stream which had a forest on the other side of it. There was a wooden sign erected at the rocks near the stream. What was odd about it was the inscription:

In four words, we do not kindly ask you weary travelers you please kindly do not destroy, flatten, or hurt grass belonging to us. You should know, say, a very great Sign to many is you emulate and perhaps are the essence of a barbarian, a putrid Green, believed to be our enemy, not a master race at all.

Both elves stared at the sign for a few moments. Finally, Zachtia said with a huff, "They certainly have bad grammar, whoever they are. Bad manners as well – who do you suppose it is?"

Aldrin was silent. He was reading it again. Something about the wording and the beginning sentence was troubling him.

Zachtia looked at him. "Is everything alright?"

"Just hold on," he said almost inaudibly. "It said 'In four words' at the beginning, but it was a paragraph. It doesn't make sense...unless..." It took him a minute to peg down his theory, but he finally laughed. "I see!"

"You see what?" asked Zachtia impatiently.

"What it's talking about! It's not talking about us at all – or being rude!"

"Well, then what does it say?"

He pointed to the beginning sentence, "It says, 'In four words'...if we just look at every fourth word on this sign it reads, 'we ask you not hurt us...say sign...you are a Green our master."

Zachtia's mouth opened and closed, as if she was about to say something. She finally shivered and said, "Right. Let's cross this river."

It was slow progress. Aldrin had learned from many years ago that one does not rush a lady elf across a stream when she is pregnant. All one does is make sure one does not fall himself, and be a stone wall for her to support herself on.

At last, they came upon the other side of the river and proceeded into the forest. It was a dense forest, but there was a little path – a clearing away of leaves and such. Brown and golden leaves made a little path. Intrigued, Aldrin followed the path with Zachtia following close behind him.

His ears and nose told him that he and Zachtia were not alone. Whispers of movement and high-speed heartbeats were everywhere around them. There could have been at least a dozen or so creatures in those woods. The creatures had a very odd way of spying on them, though: they would come a ways close to them, then scamper off as another took their places, always walking forward.

Finally, the two elves came upon a clearing, and in that clearing stood about a dozen of the creatures that had been spying on them:

They were Yellow elves; as thin and sometimes as toned as all the other colors, but so short that they could have been mistaken for children. They all wore yellow attire, their attire varying in styles. Some of them had hats on, but all had small knives in their hands. Everyone had a tension about them, as if frightened at the aspect of fighting.

Zachtia and Aldrin towered over them. Finally, Aldrin spread his arms in a messianic fashion and said in semi-dramatic fashion, "The word is…*sign*."

That was effective immediately; all the elders of the group promptly sheathed their daggers. "Thank gu'dness," said one with a frock of white hair, "I was wonderin' if I would have to run again…I don't think I could do that after ol' these years and my bad knee."

"I'm glad you didn't have to push yourself," said Aldrin, smiling warmly and bending slightly to accommodate the Yellow elf. "We're trying to get to a city, but have grown tired and hungry."

"We can banish both feelings from ya!" said the Yellow, beaming. He looked at Zachtia, and his expression suddenly showed his nervousness. "Masta' Green…" he began softly.

"Aldrin," said the Green.

"Masta' Aldrin," began the Yellow again, stepping a little closer to Aldrin's ear, "Have ya noticed your travel'n partner's choice of attire color?"

"Yes, she's a Red…one of the survivors of a Purple raid."

"Purple!" squeaked the Yellow, his eyes darting. "Are they *close?*"

"They weren't following us," said Aldrin reassuringly. "I should know."

"Yes…yes, of course, Masta' Aldrin." The Yellow's eyes fell on Zachtia once again. "Are ya…protecting a Red?"

"I…am protecting a lady," said Aldrin.

"Oh, well, um, because…we could make sure you are travel'n alone, without a Red at your ba — ack!"

Aldrin's hand had snaked out and caught the Yellow's shirt collar and had now pulled him to where the Green could have bitten off the Yellow's nose. "The only thing that you will be making sure of when dealing with her is that she is as comfortable as me, if not more so, do you understand?"

"Eep…yes, Masta' Aldrin, yes, I-I-I-I understand," the Yellow squeaked and Aldrin let go of him. He brushed himself off with an air of confidence – made all the more ridiculous by his quivering. "Well, then Masta' Aldrin and…Mistress –?"

"Zachtia," said the Red elf, finding the recent events quite informative.

"Both of ya can dine with us this evenin'!" said the Yellow. "I'm Bakyr, the lead'a o' this humble tribe, and I'll be your host!"

The rest of the small troop readily agreed.

A little Yellow girl with a small flower perched in her hair tentatively beckoned them forward before darting through the forest on the trail, the rest of the children catching up with her with excited whispers and laughs.

"Follow us, Masta' Green," said Bakyr. "We'll show you the way. The children will let the rest o' the village know of our comin' and put up two full sized chairs at the Community Table."

Aldrin was intrigued. "Community Table?" he asked.

"Yea, for suppa we all pitch in to feed the community o' our village," the Yellow elf explained, walking at a quick pace – for him – so that the two full-sized elves wouldn't have to creep along. "Sometimes we ask for visitors to bring a salad, but see'n you weren't... uh, Masta' Green?"

Aldrin had been watching the road unfold before them, but he had also been looking around, peering into the underbrush of the forest. He spied another road, unused for a long time. He immediately turned onto it and started walking it. Now he had stopped at Bakyr's question, seeing that no one else was taking the route. "I think this is the main road, isn't it?" he asked, pointing in front of him. "Clearly it hasn't been used in a while, but it's a straight path with a dip or two, and I can see a little clearing. Maybe." He pointed to the road everyone else was on. "That one twists and turns."

Zachtia looked at him and then at Bakyr. "Are you leading us astray?" She asked Bakyr with a scowl.

"Not int-tentionally, my-my lady," blustered the Yellow. "This is the path that we've always taken, but…" he walked back to where Aldrin stood and peered down the path himself. "That *is* the clearin'," he said softly. "All this time, it looks like we could'a saved about five minutes of walkin'."

"Maybe it's because you're so used to leading enemies on the longer path while the scouts tell the village?" asked Aldrin kindly, wanting to help the old man save face. "I can understand what a force habit is."

"Could we use this route, then?" asked the Red in their midst with a hint of impatience. "I've done quite a lot of walking today, especially with this baby."

"Yes'm, certainly!" replied Bakyr quickly, and hurried onwards on the old, main path.

Aldrin waved Zachtia forwards. "Let me know if you need help," he said softly.

"I'll do that," said Zachtia in a flat tone that Aldrin couldn't place whether it was agreeable or sarcastic. "Maybe you could help me a little more with what I'm supposed to expect."

"Well, a tastefully developed palate that is ten times more developed than their courage, if I remember correctly," said Aldrin with a chuckle. "Artistic peoples, though a lot of times they copied off of the masters. Wonderful listeners, though wonderful talkers too."

"Oh, like the Greens?" asked the Red with a sardonic smile. "No wonder you all got along." Her face scrunched in minor pain and Aldrin reached for her elbow for fear that she was stumbling. She shook her head. "I'm fine," she said with a slight groan in her tone. "Just thankful that this is a shorter route, I gotta use the tree…

A Warrior's Code

Chapter 4

Soon the two elves came to Bakyr at the edge of the entranceway to the village. A long-forgotten gate, camouflaged half with bushes and half with age sat open in front of him. He gestured them on. "Welcome to our village," he said. His voice had a warmness about it that hadn't been in the forest, as if coming home was coming back to a fortified city.

Zachtia and Aldrin walked through the gate into the small clearing. Aldrin immediately was looking around and taking in all the sights, which weren't a lot given that the forest became thick again about a hundred feet before them. He heard running water – a fast flowing river coming from the uphill incline to the left. It would have run straight through the clearing except near the beginning of the village – which Aldrin could just make out a long way up to the left of him – a large ditch split the river into three streams, the main way covered by large slabs of stones down the middle of the clearing.

He didn't see housing for a few moments as he took everything in. He then saw the housing and whistled just as Zachtia asked, "Where are your tents or houses? You said it was a village."

"Look up and look closely," said her Green protector softly, and she did so and quietly gasped.

In the trees were what looked like giant wasp nests, painted and shaded in such a way that they faded into the background of the trees unless one was looking for them. Aldrin could now pick out doors, windows, and ladders carved or built directly into the tree trunk itself and then molded to where it looked natural. Aldrin also spied narrow tubes, which looked like vines but were actually carved out of wood, snaking up the tree trunks and spreading throughout the village. "Most impressive," he said, thinking of the possibilities they would be used for.

"Dairlo would like this camp," Zachtia said. "Tidy, and your enemies would pass right under you without a single thought. Very practical."

Bakyr blushed with all this praise. "Really, Masta' and Mistress, you're too kind. A lo'of it we got from Green concepts and designs."

Zachtia looked at Aldrin, impressed. "Your people thought of this?"

"Apparently so," said the Green with a shrug. "Though it's the first time I've heard of it."

The same little girl Yellow with the flower in her hair ran up to Bakyr. "Suppah is almost ready, sir," she said with that same lilting accent. Aldrin had noticed that Zachtia's was like it, though thinner; much less pronounced. While hers sounded more regal, Bakyr's people's accents sounded more cut and dry. "Endia is eager to meet everyone."

"Tell her she'll see them at the table," grunted Bakyr with a weariness in his voice that Aldrin noted. Maybe Endia was his wife?

Bakyr was about to walk off with them in tow when Aldrin stopped him. He had suddenly remembered Zachtia's minor crisis. "Where's your, uh," he tried to think of a better word, or a word that the Yellows would use.

Fortunately for Zachtia, the Red beat him to it. "Where is your 'tree'?" she asked bluntly.

For a moment, Bakyr's face was blank. "My tree is one of the main ones… along this way," he said starting to point over to the right. He saw Zachtia's scowl deepen and his face lit up with recognition. "Oh, our 'tree', yes!"

"Yes," said Aldrin, giving up. "Where is it?"

At the response of "We don't have one," Zachtia stepped forward with some severity. "Don't play games," she said in a low voice, "with a pregnant Red with a bladder that's constantly being kicked. Where *is* it?"

Bakyr's face went pasty and he pointed back towards the left. "Mistress Zachredia – Redchia, uh, Miss Red, I only meant that we don't simply skulk behind a tree, we have a pot room!"

(Which was of course disguised as a tree but Aldrin wasn't going to step in to point that out.)

"The larger, base structure with the green ivy," instructed Bakyr. "Mind you close the door, though!" he added as Zachtia quickly waddled off. "It smells like death in there!"

Zachtia paused only for a second before starting again.

Supper was ready ten more minutes later, just in time for the table to be constructed. Aldrin watched with fascination as from different homes came different parts and sections of the table, while down the road from what appeared to be a termite mound there opened up a door and Yellows with trays and pots of food came up the underground steps. No sooner had the table's parts been slotted into place that a large piecemeal cloth was set over it and the furnishings were put out. Obeying Green protocols of etiquette, Aldrin watched and let all the ladies sit down first – which there were around twenty, not counting the children – and then he sat next to Bakyr. He noticed that one of the ladies – the one with crisp, strawberry-blonde hair – was looking at him curiously and beaming while the others attended more to each other with quick glances at him.

He rose again when Zachtia came up to the table, a wry and nauseated expression on her face.

Aldrin pulled out her chair for her. "You alright?" He asked.

"I hope to the Creator they don't serve mashed potatoes," the Red elf groaned. "He said it smelled like death, didn't say which *stage*, ugh."

Aldrin grimaced sympathetically. "I think we can agree to be concise on that," he muttered, looking at the wooden cutlery and plates set before him.

"Wasn't going to go any further," groaned Zachtia again, licking her lips.

The first course was salad with cheese and some type of dressing mixed in. The second was a small bowl of soup, which they had an abundance of choice to choose from. Aldrin took a meaty, potato soup while Zachtia chose a more reasonable vegetable soup.

Then the meat course came in the middle of their soup course. Aldrin guessed at once forest'fullo, an arboreal, cattle animal that was common in these kinds of woods. He was chewing happily through this course when he could no longer keep his curiosity to himself. That one little lady was still looking curiously at him and had almost missed her mouth with her fork on a couple occasions.

"So, who's that young lady?" He asked Bakyr, twitching his fork in her direction.

She reddened shyly and looked down at her meal.

Bakyr made a sound that was between a huff and a sigh. "That's mi'daughter, Endia."

So Endia was his daughter. He wondered where Bakyr's wife was. "I judge her to be around 60 years old," Aldrin guessed.

"Sixty-five, Masta' Green, a foolish girl," Bakyr replied. "She's marrying age, but no one wants her here."

Aldrin looked surprised at the young lady. It couldn't be her looks that kept people away. In her own right, though with the shortness she could be readily mistaken for a little girl, she was very pretty. "Oh?" He asked.

"You see, Masta' Green, we don' encourage, uh, courage," Bakyr stated. "But not only is she very brave for a Yellow – which sets a bad example being the daughter of a chief, huh! – she also is bold. And she didn't get the accent."

Aldrin blinked. "That comes from birth?" *Blood Memory* was something he had read in books and he saw the application. He didn't think accents would transfer, though.

"Yes, but her accent comes from her mother," Bakyr sniffed. A touch of wistfulness in his voice confirmed Aldrin's fears.

"You raise her by yourself?" he asked quietly.

"Yah," replied the Yellow with the same quietness. "But she has her mother's voice. It's like a living memory for me, bring'n me both pain and everlastin' joy." He smiled, a smile of memories being dusted off and the covers looked at before being put back on the shelf unopened.

Aldrin thought it wise to change the subject. "You said no one here wants her, as in they wish her to leave or-?"

"Ah, no, not at all, Masta Aldrin," said Bakyr with a chuckled-out sigh. "No, she leads a lo'of our hunting parties and is good with the children. No, I mean tha' I did a survey for this upcomin' Gan Hop. You would love our Gan Hop, Masta' Green, ya really would."

Also known as The Matchmaking Dance, remembered Aldrin. "And you did a survey?" He asked with a chuckle. "That's a bit of... forward thinking."

"I'm a coward, Masta' Green," said Bakyr factually, "but I'm also a father and wish the wellbein' o'my daughter." For a moment, his eyes fell on Aldrin thoughtfully, as if reaching into his mind with his hand and rummaging through the Green's qualifications.

Aldrin stopped that. "Don't ask," he said firmly. "I'm not interested." He looked at the young woman now talking with someone across from her and smiling childishly bright.

"I hope she finds someone," muttered Zachtia from beside him. He had almost forgotten she was there during the talk. "She sounds very interesting."

"Yes, she does," agreed Aldrin thoughtfully as the snappleberry pies were brought out.

An hour of eating and, much to Zachtia's consternation, talking about everything from fishing to ancient history passed, and the table was taken apart, the dishes and leftovers taken underground, and some musical instruments were brought out.

For a few hours more, Bakyr and a few others sang old, jaunty songs about humorous hunting trips, failed construction builds, and weird times in their family histories. For the Red, it was very strange. The Red Tribe did on occasion bring out instruments as well, but their songs were of battles and tales of mythical heroes. But she did enjoy a few of the tunes and the lyrics made her chuckle a few times.

Soon, darkness crept into the forest and the Yellow elves began scampering like squirrels back to their homes.

… except for Bakyr and Endia. Bakyr showed them a series of three tight-knit trees, which turned out to be a building, whose door was opened by the pocket indent of the outer tree. Inside were two beds with a table between the heads of them, and a walking space about an elf's width between.

Endia hung behind. Zachtia thought also she could sense a yearning still.

Zachtia knew the pining of a woman's heart, even at that age. Dairlo met her when she was around 90 and they hadn't been apart since their third meeting.

I'm confident your husband will be waiting for you.

She pursed her lips and forced herself to dwell on the present.

Bakyr was talking, "…your beds are covered with hart-skin blankets and linens, delicately crafted pillows, made from the finest rabbit skin and stuffed with runpaca wool."

"Runpaca?" asked Zachtia.

"It's a camel like creature, but the size of a small forest buffalo," explained Aldrin. "Known for its mane and textured skin, the runpaca is a great source of…" he trailed off when the Red gave him a look. "Eh…good food, warm clothing."

"Tell me," commented Zachtia, hands on her hips and a little smile on her face, "was the word 'brief' in your vocabulary before you met me?"

"We were 'debriefed' in the Bacht Division," said Aldrin evenly.

"I had no doubt about that," shot back Zachtia.

Bakyr continued, a little uncomfortable with the situation, "Ehhh, I can give you a wakeup call fo' breakfast — we can have a community breakfast just fo' you, I'm sure ev'ryone would be happy t' help."

"I'd like that very much," said Aldrin with a smile, his teeth white in the moonlight. He looked over at Zachtia and tilted his head. "Would you like that, Zachtia?"

"Yes," the Red forced herself to say. The thought of more talking made her internally groan, but it was the thought of one more heavy meal before wondering when her next one would be that outweighed it. "I look forward to it."

"Thank you, Masta' and Mistress," Bakyr said with a quick bow. "I'll make sure ev'ryone knows. G'night, I'll be putt'n the lights out soon."

Aldrin nodded and looked at Endia. "Have a good night, Endia," he said with a smile.

"Goodnight, Master Green," she said with a dip of her head. She looked at Zachtia. "Goodnight, Mistress Red." She took two steps back and then caught up with Bakyr, who was walking to the other end of the village to extinguish the lamps.

"She *doesn't* have the accent," observed Zachtia, watching them go and then stepping inside.

"From what Bakyr told me, that's due to Blood Memory," offered Aldrin, stepping inside as well and closing the door. There was a long board on a swivel on the door to lock it, but because he knew that Bakyr was going be their morning alarm, he left it unlocked.

Zachtia noticed a rope-controlled pully system that pushed a slat out above the window, most likely to keep out the rain. Noticing the spattering of leaves that were already on her bed, she pulled the rope, pushing the slat out, making sure no further leaves would accompany her to sleep. "Blood Memory?" she asked, brushing off the leaves.

Aldrin began, "It's the theory that-"

Zachtia had sat down on the bed and now raised a finger. "Succinctly, you promised," she warned tiredly. The Red got into a lying position that was the least uncomfortable as she listened. The Green cleared his throat, "-both physical features as well as mental features can be passed down through the family's blood. She got her hair color from her mother, and she also got her accent."

Zachtia rubbed her belly thoughtfully, looking down as if through to the life inside her. The child had gotten the notion that it was bedtime and was fidgeting less. Wonderful. "Her mother died in childbirth, then?" she surmised. "Or soon after."

"That's my thought," replied Aldrin. "Complications." He looked hard at the Red's protruding belly. "Of which none I can detect."

"Don't look too hard, you might lose an eye," grumped Zachtia under her breath, but she had to be grateful to a point. "You a medicinal man as well?"

"I did my research," said Aldrin slowly. He was about to say something more but he trailed off. "If you're ready to sleep, I'll put out the light," he said instead, climbing into his own bed.

"Yes, please," Zachtia said, closing her eyes. Soon the light in front of them disappeared and she smelled the faint smell of candle smoke.

"Goodnight, Zachtia," said Aldrin. A rustle of the rough sheets. Was he cold on this warm night?

"Goodnight, Aldrin," said Zachtia. She counted her breaths to a hundred and soon after fell asleep.

A Warrior's Code

Chapter 5

Zachtia opened her eyes and stretched, looking out the window at the glorious view of the little village of the Yellow tribe. She was not too sure how long she had been asleep, but she knew she had at least slept the entire night. The bed was supremely comfortable – much better than the fold-up planks the Reds slept on in their encampments. From the window, she could see clear, blue skies, a few birds and perhaps a dragon or two were flying high above the treetops.

She could stay here forever…but she knew that was not possible.

She looked over at Aldrin who was in a bed across the room. He was still sound asleep, on his stomach, head on the pillow and arms under the pillow. His face was relaxed more than what it usually was.

He listened to the sweet whispering of the air as he staggered along the dirt-trodden road. He clutched at his arm in pain, wincing as blood seeped through the wound of the arrow shot.

But Aldrin had been victorious. He looked at the sunrise and smiled against the bombardment of burning and spiking shooting through his body; it was a red sun.

…and then he heard something: a sound that he wished not to hear – and it was coming from his camp!

It was screaming! Not just any screaming, but the screaming of his wife, Malendire! He tore across the landscape, his elven nose picking up the horrifying smell of smoke and burning materials; burning flesh. As he neared his camp, he saw what he thought to be snowfall – but it was in the middle of the dry season! It was ash – ash from his camp!

He got to the hill that parted his town from the landscape – and he stopped.

There was the town; besieged and fallen – torn apart and scattered about. He looked around for any sign of life, but from the hilltop he could not see anything. The screaming he heard had ceased…it had stopped the moment he reached the hilltop.

With a deep breath and a gut-wrenching knot in his stomach, he descended into the town.

"Malendire!" he called out to the one of his desires. He called out again, this time to his entire family, "Malendire! Mayberry! Fennec! Please no…don't do this to me…" He trudged on and on…looking at the horrible landscape; looking at the burned homes and flags; looking at the burning and rotting bodies that plagued the streets.

Tark, a friend of the Green, was sitting hunched up against a tree, his head sawed in half and signature blade through his heart. Barrak, an acquaintance – his corpse was found in a tree.

…and then Aldrin saw the sight he had seen in nightmares but now it was all too real:

His home had been flattened…and his wife had been tied with her hands to the stake where they would tie the dog. Aldrin's children had been tied to their mother, one on each side. Last of all, they had been burned to a crisp.

His legs suddenly could not hold his weight anymore and he dropped to his knees. He wailed and cried out! He crawled like an infant to his smoldering wife…her eyes were closed. Those eyes that would look up at him in love…those eyes that would laugh when she herself would just smile and shake her head at him. His children had been clinging to their mommy…wanting to know one final time if everything would be alright.

He suddenly heard a chattering sound…and slowly turned about.

There, coming up to him, were the heads of every Red that he had killed in the battle. Each one of them were rotten and stank.

Aldrin, his disgust drowned out by fury, shouted at them, *"You did this!"*

The heads grinned wickedly. "Your fate will be the same," said the first one in the crowd.

"Aldrin..."

He turned around to his name spoken by his angel.

Nothing had changed – except her eyes. Her eyes were open and open with such a horrific wideness that Aldrin nearly wretched. Those eyes looked at him and grew sad as she said, "...why couldn't you save us?" Suddenly she screamed his name, her mouth opening into a maw and he turned back just in time to see the many heads of his enemies swarming around him...and jumping –!

I'm confident your husband will be waiting for you.

She remembered him saying that and she bit her lip. What if her husband was dead? What if she was all alone when she went into Scarlesh? Her baby...how would she provide for her child?

"Aldrin!" she cried, in an upset panic, wrapping her arms around herself.

She had no idea what an impact she would have on him by saying that word – she found out instantly when he came up swinging! His knife was in hand in case of a late-night tackle and now it was flashing in the sunlight. Zachtia shrieked as the Green elf careened out of his bed, eyes wide as saucers. *"Malendire!"* he screeched as his eyes rolled in his head, his brow furrowed, the rest of his body as tense as a whip, his breaths coming as furious pants.

He looked at Zachtia. "No...just..." his lower lip quivered and he fought to keep his composure. He looked away from the elf, she wondering what was going to happen next.

He started to relax. It took him about a minute to do so, his breaths slowly becoming deeper.

He sat down slowly, the hand which had white-knuckle gripped the handle of the blade now almost let it go. He looked back at the Red elf, and when he did, he said in a very, very quiet voice, "Yes, Zachtia?"

"…how do you know my husband will be at Scarlesh?"

He looked down. She looked closer and saw to her astonishment that he was crying. "I'm sorry…" she said.

"It's not you," began Aldrin, but he sighed and with a tearful hoarse voice he amended, "It's not *entirely* you. It's just…my wife would call out the same way if she were in trouble."

"What happened to your wife?" asked Zachtia softly, sincerely.

The Green looked at her and her breath caught in her throat. There was horrific sorrow in his eyes – one emotion that she had never seen from him. "The Red Tribe killed her without provocation." He went on, his breath catching several times: "After the Battle of Redblood I went back to my encampment, injured, exhausted, but victorious. I…was nearing the encampment – about half a mile away – when I smelled smoke…and ashes were floating on the breeze like snowfall.

"I began running, my heart caught in my throat…when I got there…*mh*…when I got there the entire camp had been decimated. Our flags were burning, homes smashed…bodies burned to the skeletons."

Aldrin took a deep breath his tears flowing freely and his speech almost unintelligible, "…I searched the remains…for my wife…and I buried her…and my two children…where our home had been…" His story ended and his shoulders wracked with his sobs.

Zachtia did not know what to do…she was a Red and she knew it all too well. But she did know one thing: "Aldrin…I am so sorry…my husband told me of Redblood…it was a very good battle, just not for the Reds…" she bit her lip. "…he also told me of a plan to wipe out an encampment. When I heard it was just women and children I…I told him it was a terrible plan."

She looked down. "…I don't know how that was supposed to make you feel better –"

"It did."

She slowly lifted her eyes and saw that Aldrin had turned to face her. "It tells me that you're not one of them…" He smiled slightly through his tears and said softly, "Ever considered becoming a Green?"

She smiled slightly and said, "Ah, well…I couldn't talk that much…besides, my husband wouldn't let…me." Now it was her turn to cry. She cried softly and said, "Oh Aldrin…what if Dairlo is dead? My husband…"

She watched Aldrin as he slowly got off of his bed and sat beside her on her bed. "Zachtia," he said, "I give it my best hope that your husband will be at Scarlesh. There's always that chance. I have been taking you the route I know to Scarlesh…he might be taking a different route." He grasped her hand. "I swear to protect you, Zachtia, Red Elf, at least until we get to Scarlesh, and on the off-chance that your husband is not there…I will protect you until we find him."

Zachtia looked at him…and put her arms around him and wept.

Before meeting Aldrin, Zachtia had only embraced two men: her brother and her husband. She had always felt that she became more personal with a man if she embraced him. Now when she had looked at Aldrin…she saw the protectiveness of her husband and the love of her brother. Green or Red, he was an elf that meant more to her now than he did when she saw him towering over her on that stormy night.

She felt his arms slowly settle onto her and her crying gradually died down. "I'm sorry...I...I'm just glad I have a...brother to look after me."

"I know..." she heard in her ear. "I'm glad I have a sister to finally let out everything that has been bottled up."

There was a knock on the door and both elves turned to see the door open and Bakyr's voice rang joyously, "I hope I'm not coming in at a bad time, but breakfast is on the ta –"

He stopped halfway in the doorway for a moment as he ogled the two elves. "Ah...eh...apparently I have come in at a bad time...I'll-I'll-I'll-I'll check back later..."

As he left, Zachtia looked at Aldrin. "Should I explain to him, 'brother', or will you?"

Chapter 6

It took about fifteen minutes to make it clear to Bakyr – and the elves that he had talked to about what he saw – that Aldrin was not involved with Zachtia, and even then, it seemed that they were not quite convinced.

Breakfast consisted of scrambled eggs in giant omelets, which Zachtia had never had prepared for her. She enjoyed the egg-wrapped cheese, meat, and vegetable delicacy and asked for the recipe to prepare for Dairlo.

Afterwards, when the table had been put away, Aldrin thought it best that they leave.

Since Aldrin and Zachtia had nothing to carry, they started on their way to the other end of the forest. Bakyr said the straight shot would lead them out of the forest into a clearing which the scouts had many a time spied upon but never passed into. They had just stepped through the first set of trees, when a female voice rang out behind them, "Wait! I want to join you!"

Zachtia and Aldrin turned around and saw that it was Bakyr's daughter who had spoken. Endia had been running towards them and had now come to a halt in front of them. "Please," Endia said, trying to catch her breath, "I...don't want to stay here. I want to go exploring with you...I want..." she took a deep breath to steady herself. "Whoof...pardon me, but I'm seeing sparkles..."

As he had seen at the table but now with a clearer view, Aldrin could see she was about four feet tall with strawberry-blonde hair, but now it was encircled with a band of silver to keep it out of her eyes, and in her hand, she had a sword about half her height.

"Are you sure, Endia?" he asked. "It's probably going to be dangerous."

There was no mistaking the un-Yellow sparkle in Endia's eyes as she nodded. "Master Green," she said eagerly, "that is what I have dreamed of getting into; I wish for adventure – for danger!"

Suddenly Bakyr's voice called out, "And ye'll *still* have t' dream for it, daughta'!" His brogue had become thicker in his vexation and he grabbed her arm as if to haul her back from the dangers of the unknown.

Endia gave a cry of despair. "Father, please!" she said. "I'm not just some child!"

"No, yur no' ju'*some* child, I'll give you that!" said Bakyr, looking her straight in her eye. He huffed and said in a more controlled tone, "You are me daughter, Endia. You are a Yellow elf; we don' get involved in anyone else's business. We serve the Greens – and tha' 'sall. They protect us because we cannae protect ourselves."

"They can't protect you anymore," said Aldrin softly. "They are all dead except for me and on the Council."

That had a definite effect on the Yellow leader. His grip was released from Endia and he started to sputter and stagger backwards. "Dead? Greens…d-dead? Wh-who's gonna p-p-p-p…"

Endia had to catch her father as he lost the strength in his knees. "I think you might want to sit down," she said and he mumbled a reply. She looked at Aldrin. "You better not be lying just to get him riled," she shot with protective coldness in her voice.

"It's true," Zachtia replied for Aldrin. "My… husband's army wiped the last encampment out." *Though not his division,* she specified silently.

Endia's sword had been dropped in the efforts to catch Bakyr and was immediately taken back up. "Then your husband is a villain," she seethed. "What manner of elf are you to marry a creature who would kill innocents?" Endia's head whipped over to her Green protector. "And you – why do you *really* tarry with this Red?"

Zachtia was about to give the girl a verbal whipping when she realized what kind of tactic she was using. She was using the same tactic verbally as an owl does physically when it ruffles its feathers to make itself seem larger than it actually was. The angry voice was protective, not so much angry. And yet there was genuine anger in that voice. Maybe she had thoughts that this wonderful Green wasn't as she thought him to be?

Her father's voice gurgled from the ground, "Greens...Reds...Purples...maybe we could...dig holes...underground...people...mole-people...mole-mole-mole-"

"Endia," said Aldrin, "Get your father into his hut and splash some cool water on his face. I'll explain after you do."

With a glare, Endia complied, hefting her father in her arms and carried him while he still said the word "mole" repeatedly.

While she was gone, Aldrin huffed out a sigh. "This is just getting better and better," he muttered. "First she wants to join us then she wants to kill us then she wants to listen – what's next?"

Zachtia rubbed her boulder of a belly thoughtfully. "Well, I don't see a reason why we couldn't take her along. I wouldn't mind another protector."

"Indeed, but a Green with a Yellow and a Red – that's going to look incredibly bizarre...not that a Green with a Red is normal, either," said Aldrin.

Zachtia smirked and shook her head.

Endia came from her father's hut. "With any luck," she said, sounding a little more compliant, "he'll come around after you're gone." She sat about five feet from them, cross-legged, and said,

"Tell on, Master Green. What's your story?" Sitting down like this she really did look like a child.

Aldrin explained everything, from his camp being decimated right to when both elves arrived at the Yellow's encampment. All the while, Endia listened intently, never speaking a word except to ask the occasional question, usually for clarification. One aspect of the Yellow was that they were very poor at hiding emotions, especially in the facial area. Aldrin noticed that Endia was becoming more sympathetic with the two elves.

When Aldrin had finished his tale, Endia nodded slowly, taking in the information, and said softly, "Well…I hope you both have a safe journey." She began to walk away.

"Endia," called Aldrin. "We see no problem with you coming along."

Endia whipped around. "But my father does," she said angrily. "And I won't disobey my father. I'm brave – not foolish."

"Then go talk to him," said Aldrin. "Reason with him."

"You've seen how that turns out," Endia huffed. "…why don't *you* reason with him?"

"Me?" Aldrin started…but then after giving it some thought he said more to himself, "Yes, I see your point. I, being a Green, will instigate a fa…"

Again, he got a mildly amused look from Zachtia and he summed up, "I'll talk to him."

Aldrin had to wait until the elder had regained his senses. He then sat down and had a long, difficult conversation with him. Not that the elder was not compliant (indeed, for a man that nearly lost his mind, he was taking the conversation fairly well,), but the main problem was Bakyr kept dazing off.

Finally, Aldrin had him convinced that because there were no Greens left except for himself and the Council, Endia would be the safest with Aldrin. She would also learn her place as servant and knowledge finder, and perhaps one day become the protector of the Yellow's encampment.

In the span of five hours after they wanted to leave, the group of now three elves left the encampment. Aldrin was intrigued by Endia about an hour out. For a Yellow that had the wanton bravery of a Red she was still extremely informative and *very* smart.

He asked her about her history and childhood, trying but not entirely succeeding to ground the fact in his mind that she wasn't as much a child as she looked with her big, innocent looking eyes and slightly goofy grin.

"I grew up in the village," began Endia. "You could say the entire village raised me, not just my father. They all taught me how to write, to read, to hunt... but I learned how to do a lot of stuff on my own because they were too afraid to show me and I could never understand why. Father always said it was the way of the Yellow to scout and fly and tell, but... I'm different." She ran her hand through her hair. "I'm an inch taller than the rest of the females of my village, for one thing."

"I saw that, and that intrigued me," offered Aldrin with a soft smile. "So, if I may make a deduction, you never knew your mother?"

Endia slowed her pace and, getting a grunt from Zachtia, Aldrin did so as well. "Father always talks in glowing terms about my mother," the Yellow said in a quiet voice. "About her being firm yet so kind and gentle. And she was taller than all the others too," she added with what sounded like a touch of pride. "He rarely talks about her otherwise, if at all."

Aldrin nodded thoughtfully.

"And I have these memories..." Endia realized she was dragging the group and picked up her pace. "And yet I dunno, it's like I've heard so much about her that I can almost picture what she looks like."

"A lot of elf children get false memories from the feelings and thoughts around them when they were born," said Aldrin, his eyes sparkling at the thought. "It's because minds of infants are practically reaching out for information on how to live and subconsciously wanting to know about this strange new world."

Endia was silent for a while. "My mother died in childbirth," she stated after a while with some emotional distance. "I have a ... well, I can't call it a nightmare, but a disturbing dream about it. It shifts erratically from different viewpoints and it's all muddled and-" she shuddered. "Disturbing."

Aldrin tentatively squeezed her shoulder and nodded sympathetically. "I have those too, though that's not something about I want to get into..."

Endia nodded quickly and offered brightly, "How about theories on botanical studies?"

Zachtia mildly noted to, on her next adventure, bring a strip of binding cloth or find a clothwrapp fir to peel so that if she found another Yellow, she could bind its mouth shut. Now that Aldrin and Endia had gotten on a subject of scientific studies – of which the Reds rarely were experts on – they almost hadn't even stopped to take a breath. On and on Aldrin and Endia talked, using words about seven syllables long in sentences about ten words across, and basically acting like children who were hyped up on Zinta-leaf extract.

Finally, Aldrin noticed Zachtia's cringe and asked, "Are you alright, Zachtia?"

"I need to find a clothwrapp tree," she muttered under her breath.

Endia walked a little faster until she was beside the Red elf. "She looks mildly exasperated," she said. "You can tell with the imbalance of color in –"

"Yes! I'm exasperated!" said Zachtia, throwing up her hands, "I have finally gotten used to Aldrin's talking but now to have both of you bantering like a bunch of hyper preliminary teenagers is almost unbearable!" She looked at Aldrin with a pleading expression. "Aldrin, *please*, could you tone it down?"

Aldrin had been taken aback at first, but then he nodded slowly and said, "Of course…how…foolish of me. I had forgotten about your dislike of…mounds of talking."

"It's a little unhealthy!" cried Endia, looking at Zachtia with concern. "You should probably read up on Magistrate Da'an's 'Lantern Into Knowledge' literature. It's a very good read!"

"Perhaps I will," said Zachtia, fighting the urge to roll her eyes, "But until then, I would rather keep walking in mild silence, alright?"

Both the Yellow and Green nodded and Zachtia continued forward…but not without hearing Endia whisper, "…I still want to discuss Elanticon's Requirem of Polygonal Side-Distribution sometime…"

The rest of the hour, for Zachtia at least, was quite peaceful. Even the Green and Yellow had to admit, it was…profitable, keeping with one's own thoughts. Though, there was a time during the third hour that Aldrin had to talk because his thoughts were getting too depressing. It was in this hour that both the Red and Green elves saw Endia's true gentility and compassion. She was very kind to Aldrin, listening to him and her voice lost the edge that it had had with him when she scolded him at the camp. Aldrin, in turn, was gracious to her and gave her the answers to her questions…but also was gracious to Zachtia and kept his voice low, much to her approval.

They traveled on, crossing another river via a wooden bridge, down into a valley, across a plain of wood-colored grass, until they finally came to a city.

Endia looked at it as they were drawing nearer. "Is this Scarlesh?" she asked.

"No," Aldrin said, sounding a little unnerved, "This is Fyreton, her sister city."

"So, it's a Red city?" asked Zachtia, relieved. "Finally…I can ask around to see if my husband has been seen."

Aldrin gritted his teeth and surveyed the city once again. "About a mile deep…half a mile across – more like a town than a city."

He got a glare from Zachtia and a giggle from Endia. "Endia and I will camp out here then. You can go in and get supplies and information and we'll meet you on the other side --"

"Hold on," cried Zachtia. "I'm not going in there alone! No woman is allowed to be without a male accompaniment or at least three more females…it's the policy of the Red cities. Keeps the lady population safe from any…disturbances."

Aldrin grunted. "We certainly don't want any of those…but I'm a Green, if you'll recall."

The Red made a face at him. "I don't think I could forget it, Aldrin."

The Yellow nodded ascent, "So you probably don't have to be reminded of what I am, I presume?"

Before Zachtia could retort, Aldrin cleared his throat. "So...what do you suggest? Walking in there with a Yellow and a Green would be...inadvisable."

Endia piped up, "The odds of our going into that city and coming out without incidents are 42,730-to-1...extremely inadvisable, if you ask me."

"Well, if you haven't learned this about us Reds, let me tell you," Zachtia said, setting her jaw, "we don't count the odds. Let's go."

With no argument to be made to that response, the Yellow and Green elves nodded to each other and joined her in crossing the threshold to the city.

Chapter 7

Every eye was on the group – at least that is what it felt like to Aldrin and Endia as they followed the brazen Zachtia down the cobblestone road. The women quieted their haggling at the vendors and started whispering amongst themselves. Younger men suddenly had the urge to check the weapons on their persons while older men just gazed on, some of them making back-in-my-day comments.

Endia was thoroughly fascinated by the whole concept of "city" …or "town", for that matter. Her childlike appearance gave credit to the innocence she portrayed as she was practically led by the hand through the city, soaking in all the "sights".

Aldrin, on the other hand, felt trapped. He felt for his bow at his back that was not there and found, to his relief, that it was still strung to his back. He felt the cloak that was not there resting on his shoulders and fingered at its clasp. To the passerby it would have looked strange, him rubbing something invisible at his neck.

It certainly was to Zachtia. Leaning in a little, she asked softly, "Problem with your shirt collar?"

"You remember, on the night that we met, I gave you my cloak to use as a pillow?" asked Aldrin.

"Yes, I remember," replied Zachtia, confused.

"Where is it now?"

Zachtia started to answer, then thought about it. "…I don't know," she said. "I haven't seen it since we left the forest."

"And yet, it is sitting around my shoulders right now," replied Aldrin.

"It is?" the Red elf asked.

"Yes. Also, my cap is on my head, both my bow and a quiver full of arrows are slung over my back, I have a small bag at my waist, and I have a picklock in my pocket."

Zachtia quickly scanned the first few locations and yet found nothing. "...How is that possible?" she finally asked, thoroughly confused.

"I'll explain later," replied Aldrin.

"Well, that's a first," said Zachtia, surprised.

"I'm tense, Zachtia...extremely tense." Aldrin looked uneasily at a couple of fellows that stopped their conversation to stare at the group. "Every single person that isn't blind is staring at us – at me! ...I stick out like a sore thumb – and like Endia said, the odds are against me."

Zachtia put a hand on his shoulder. "You'll be fine, Aldrin. We just need to get some supplies, find a place to rest, have a hot meal, and then we'll be out of here."

"Is that all?" asked Aldrin a little sarcastically. "Hmph, then I probably shouldn't unpack, eh?"

"What do you have to – oh never mind." Zachtia shook her head as they continued down the road. "I don't think I'll ever understand you."

They passed up a few vendors because of the looks they were giving them, but they finally saw a younger vendor and made their stop. The young woman was frightened by Aldrin at first, but when she saw that Aldrin was basically just playing the part of the silent guardian, she loosened up enough to let them buy a pillow, a couple of water canteens, and some other supplies. Aldrin slung the supplies bag around his left shoulder. "I'll make this disappear, too," he whispered to Zachtia as they left the vendor counting her coins.

"I bet you will," said Zachtia, giving her head a shake.

The Dancing Dragon Inn came complete with a dining room and serving center. Ale was flowing, people from their consciousnesses were slowly dropping…and ironically it was the most reputable Inn the group could find.

Aldrin noticed that the bartender/waitress was quite unflappable. Indeed, when she came over to their table and welcomed them to the Inn, her face was kind and calm. When he questioned the 240-some-odd brunette about it, the middle-aged elf replied, "Son, everything and everyone has come to my Inn sooner or later and I serve them all the same. As soon as you walked through that door, you ceased being a color and became what the Creator made you: an elf…no hues about it."

"…Can we take her home?" the Green elf asked in a groan to his companions and got a chuckle from their server and a mild slap on the shoulder from Zachtia. He then chuckled himself and said in his normal tone, "What's your name, Ma'am?"

"Relina, son – and my Inn needs me so, no, you can't take me home with you." She gave him a wry smile. "Sorry. Now…what'll it be?"

Before any of the group could answer, there came a strong, disgusted male voice at the other end, "Will you stop messing around with that Green's table and come to us real men?" His voice was followed by his and his table's laughter.

Relina waved them off. "Don't pay any attention to them," she said. "They're one of the wealthy families here, the head one is a noble. He's basically paid off so many officials that he can get away with anything…with that being said, I have to attend to them." She grimaced. "I'll be back as soon as I can, alright?"

She walked over to the other table and took their orders as well as quelled a few attempts to touch her. Aldrin looked approvingly – now there was at least *one* Red that did not need protecting.

She *finally* got back to them to get their orders and brought them out first – but to be fair, it was only because they were cooked first that they were served first.

Aldrin thought it was the best scrambled Panduck eggs that he had ever had, not to mention some very good toasted bread and sanberry juice. He could not enjoy it fully, though, for his attention kept averting to the "wealthy family" who was getting louder by the minute, not to mention drunker.

Indeed, Aldrin was back to being tense as the table yonder got even more rowdy. He shot a glance over at Relina at the bar and she gave them a helpless shrug. "Not allowed" she mouthed to him.

"Things are getting out of hand," Aldrin said. "We better get out of here."

He stood up and gave a quick nod to his companions and started for the door.

Immediately, the noble stood up. "Where ya going, Green?" he slurred. "We haven't prop'rly met yet."

"Aldrin, last of the Green Elves," Aldrin said briskly. "You are a wealthy elf who thinks he can get away with anything just because he has money in his pocket. Money is power, so therefore you believe you have power. Now, with the introductions out of the way, I'd rather take my leave."

The elf walked towards him with a sneer. "Not with'at kind of attitude." He looked back at the others as they stood up. "How's about we give this elf an attitude adjustment, eh?"

As the elf was turned, Aldrin quickly felt around in his pocket and pulled out what looked like a steel billy club with two handles in the middle, and when the Red elf turned back, Aldrin grasped the handles and pulled outward, the club extending into a six-foot fighting lance.

The Red looked impressed. "They said that you Greens were magical. Let's see how you do against force!"

The Red threw a left hook only to be stopped by a block of Aldrin's staff. Aldrin wrenched his staff to the left, catching his attacker's hand and slapping it away and immediately followed with a thrust of his weapon lengthwise into the Red's chest.

Another of the table rushed him, a lanky, muscular fellow. Aldrin slammed the butt of his staff into the elf's shins, making him trip, and in the middle of the elf's fall, down came the staff into the middle of his back.

Two came at him, fists swinging, they looking like brown-haired twins. Aldrin shoved his staff in between them and gave it a whirl, smacking into one's forehead and the back of the other's head.

The first elf was back on his feet, this time kicking his right foot up and catching Aldrin in the stomach. Aldrin bent over, in pain, but kept his head enough to slam his body into the Red, both going down in the process. Immediately, the Red grappled for

A Warrior's Code

Aldrin's throat but the Green slammed his head into the Red elf's nose, knocking the elf's head back with a yelp.

All this time the other patrons of the Inn stood by watching. Now that they saw that the Green had the upper hand, they rushed him. Aldrin barely had time to collapse his staff and put it in his pocket before four Red men had his hands behind his back, he himself down on his knees.

The noble, out of breath and nose bloodied and somewhat flat, staggered to his feet. He met Aldrin's gaze with a fierce glare. "Take them to jail," he seethed.

Within moments, Aldrin, Zachtia, and Endia were being forced to walk down the streets of the city, wondering how they were going to get out of *this* situation.

But Aldrin had a plan. He was not all that worried. In fact, he smirked as they passed by two elderly men as he could read on the man's lips, "Now, that's what they did back in my day."

Chapter 8

Zachtia was more livid than she had been in her life. The only thing that kept her from devolving into a savage beast and tearing her captors to pieces was the life in her womb.

But that did not keep her from trying to tear herself out of the hands of the officer and hollering, "You won't get away with this! I am a Red elf in a Red city – I am Zachtia, wife of Dairlo, commander of the Third Division! Unhand me!"

She got her wish, if to only find herself tumbling into a prison cell. She glared at the crowd as the doors shut and were locked. She immediately was back on her feet and she grasped the bars tight. "I demand to see the warden!" she snarled.

As the crowd dispersed, she glared at Aldrin and Endia who were behind her. Aldrin, for the most part, did not seem too worked up about the situation. He was sitting down, cross-legged, where he had been led and was looking up at her. Endia was sitting across from him and looked a little more nervous, but fascinated more than anything. Which did *not* help the Red's mood – in fact, it made it worse.

When she turned around, she was met with a brawny, bearded elf in a scarlet tank top, but his shoulders to his elbows were wrapped in dark red leather. Wrapped around his head were straps of the same leather, covering his left eye and his left ear – though it looked as if the ear was not there to begin with – and peeking out from under the straps Zachtia could see scars, like the ones one would get when whipped.

A Warrior's Code

He spoke, his low voice having a gravelly texture, "I am the warden of this jail, dear."

"How dare you call me –?"

"Because I know your husband, Zachtia," the man said. He looked at her with a sullen eye. "He spoke so highly of you. You were his conscience, his backbone. Why on earth are you with this Green and…is that a Yellow?"

"Endia," the female Yellow piped up. "Pleased to meet your acquaintance, warden."

The warden sneered and looked back at Zachtia. "You know the consequences for treason, Zachtia."

She rattled the bars in response. "I am not a traitor! I was pursued by a Purple elf and Aldrin came to my rescue! He's accompanying me to Scarlesh to protect me."

"Unbelievable," said the warden, putting his face in his left hand.

"It is *very* believable! He is the last of the tribe-ridden Green elves. Warden, please! I am no traitor!"

"You expect me to believe that the enemy of the Reds would seek to save the very essence of what destroyed him?"

It was at this time that Aldrin spoke up, "Yes, she does. I do too – is that so much to ask?"

The warden was quiet for a moment…but then he took a deep breath and straightened up. "No one is above the law. Any elf that is caught fraternizing with a Green elf will be sent to the nearest jail and will stay there for the rest of their life, as is the law of this town."

Zachtia shook the bars again, this time with a raging wail. "No!"

The warden shook his head. "I am so sorry, Zachtia. That's what is going to happen. Only if your husband posts your bail will you be allowed to go free." He grasped the bars himself and leaned in close. "He and I are very good friends – we fought together many times," he whispered. "I will personally send a letter to him asking for your bail. I'm not sure about your story..." He gave Aldrin and Endia a once-over. "...but I will take your word for it."

The warden straightened up and cleared his throat. "Green and Yellow, I see no reason why I cannot just lock you up here with this Red. You will spend your natural lives here as well."

Aldrin stood up. "If her husband posts bail," he said, "Would it be possible for us to be set free as well, provided he believes her story?"

"Green," huffed the warden, "You're lucky your head isn't rolling on the floor right now. This is beyond policy to let a Green even *breathe* in a jail owned by Rekton, lord of Fyreton."

("That explains a lot," said Endia under her breath.)

"And we all thought that the Yellow tribe was just a myth," continued the Red. "We have no policy against such cowards."

This time Endia gave him a glare. "How about you let me out and I show you how cowardly I am?"

The warden chuckled. "Little lady, you will have a good amount of eternity to think about what you're asking for. Believe me – eternity is much less bloody."

The warden and the guards accompanying him walked away from the cage. "Hope you all like grits," the warden called over his shoulder. "'Cause that's what you're going to get for the rest of your life, three times a day…"

Zachtia had stopped listening. She slowly backed away from the bars of the cell, biting her lip.

Aldrin started towards her. "Zachtia, I am so–"

"*It's your fault!*" The Red elf angrily pointed at him. "It's *your* fault that *we* are *in* this mess. *Your* fault that I will never see my husband again. *Your*…f-fault…" Her knees gave out and Aldrin had to scramble to catch her. As soon as she had her seat, she waved him off.

He sat cross-legged in front of her, Endia sitting across from the two, making a triangle of elves. "You're right," the Green elf said softly as tears fell down his Red companion's face. "If I hadn't saved you, you would have nothing to worry about. You wouldn't have a care in the world, what," his voice suddenly turned cold, "being torn to shreds, scattered across the Trepidation Forest and painting the trees in the shred-radius a scarlet with your innards."

Zachtia looked away from him, her face curled in a grimace. She knew it was true…but she did not want to admit it.

Aldrin spoke up again, this time a little more kindly. "Now, considering the options, I'd rather be here, having saved your life, and had finally found the *one* Red that would actually consider me a friend."

Zachtia looked at him, wiping her tears from her eyes, exhausted. "Don't make me regret that decision…and another thing – how can you be so confoundedly *calm?*"

"Because I know that your husband loves you," Aldrin said. "Because I know that...whatever the circumstances, Endia, you, and I will still be alive to figure things out...and because I know, if things go badly, how to get out of here."

Endia's eyes brightened. "I *thought* as much! What do you have in mind?"

"Well, I...hold on..." Aldrin suddenly straightened. "The warden's talking to someone..."

Endia straightened up too. "I can't hear – what are they saying?"

Zachtia was listening too. "The other elf is angry...do you suppose –?"

"Yes, yes, that at least *sounds* like that elf at the table that I inverted the nose of," Aldrin said, craning his ears. "Something about...incarceration...he's saying that he's angry that we are not being executed...warden says he – the, uh, noble – doesn't have jurisdiction or leverage on the warden's jail – good for him..."

"...oh, that got the noble riled," Endia whispered, picking up his much louder vocalizations.

Now Zachtia spoke. "He's telling the warden he'll be back...I don't like the sound of that."

Aldrin set his jaw. "Right," he said, standing up. "We'll need that plan of escape before he does."

The Red watched as he walked to the center of the room. "And that is?"

"Quiet for now..." Aldrin said, taking his pointer finger and thumb and measuring the brick in the center of the room.

"Last thing I thought I'd hear from a Green," muttered Zachtia as she watched him repeat the process with the surrounding four bricks. "Any chance you could fill me in?"

Aldrin sighed softly. "I'm going to need to do some calculating. Too tired to do it in my head…"

He walked over to the doors and peered through the bars. The warden was down the hall, about 5 cells from them. "That'll do," Aldrin said softly, walking back to the middle of the room. He concentrated, closing his eyes, and stretched his left arm down beside himself. Zachtia and Endia watched in fascination as his hand moved as if he were rummaging through something, then both lady elves gasped when he pulled his hand up and in it appeared a tablet of papyrus and an ink-filled quill pen.

It was Endia that snapped out of her shock first. "I *knew* it! I knew it could be done!" she shouted, then covered her mouth in a blush as the warden called for them to have a little less noise. "It's the 'Displacement', right?" she whispered excitedly.

"Indeed." Aldrin reached beside himself again and this time came back up with a measuring stick. "Now I can do this properly."

Zachtia jaw was still slack, eyes wide open, but then she shook her head and said, "Did I *miss* something? First you act as if it doesn't matter if we're incarcerated for life, and now you are pulling things out of – air?!"

…and then, either from the sheer overwhelming blow to her perception of reality, or the sheer exhaustion one gets from this kind of adventure…Zachtia passed out.

When she started to come to, she found she was being left out of another session of Endia and Aldrin talking in words up to seven syllables each in sentences ten words across…

"Now, did you account for Benajor's Catalytic Theorem?" Endia was asking.

"Yes, but Relinda's Disposition on Physical Application cancels that out to the seventh decimal," Aldrin replied, measuring the far wall.

"And we're just using six – got it."

Zachtia groaned and both elves looked at her. "Glad I didn't miss anything," she said.

Endia grunted. "Good morning to you too, Mrs. Red. How'd you sleep?"

The Red breathed out in another groan. "Like the rocks I'm feeling under my backside…but what did I miss? I was asleep for the entire night?"

"Indeed," Aldrin said, jotting down a figure on his papyrus tablet. "We slept for about three hours then when we heard that the warden had fallen asleep, we started measuring and calculating."

"Okay…" Zachtia said slowly, sitting up a little bit straighter. "In terms you think I'd be able to understand, I want you to explain yourselves. First, tell me how you pulled objects out of thin air, *Aldrin*, and also why you are measuring our cell."

"Speaking of which," Aldrin interjected turning to Endia, "4.593681-by-5.802341 Inlets, Endia,"

"Got it," Endia said, writing on her own tablet which apparently Aldrin had given her.

Zachtia sighed quietly and waited for them to finish writing on their tablets, come over to her, and sit down. They did so about five minutes afterward.

"Right…" Aldrin said, licking his lips. "A while back, there was a brilliant theorist/scientist named Rae Elanticon. She was incredibly intelligent (though quite absent-minded) and made some fantastic theories which were tested and reinforced by other scientists."

"One day," Endia continued, "Rae accidentally misplaced one of her scientific tools and couldn't find it anywhere. Story goes that she remembered that she had been so tired that she had to concentrate really hard on putting it on the table. Although she had checked that table a dozen times before, she went back to it, closed her eyes, and thought about picking it up. There, to her amazement, she found that although there was nothing on the table, she felt her hand grasp the tool…and when she withdrew her hand, still holding the tool, it appeared in her hand as if it had been there all along."

Aldrin took it from there. "She tried many forms of concentration – don't ask me how – and she found that concentration on the place that she would put the object would inadvertently 'displace' the object out of sight. The opposite happened when she picked up items after 'displacing' them."

"Okay, so now I get the whole 'displacement' thing…" Zachtia grimaced, "…somewhat…but how about you two measuring the place? What's that about?"

"One of Elanticon's requirems – basically, what is required for something to be truly what it is defined as – was the Requirem of Polygonal Side-Distribution," Aldrin explained. "If we can get the calculations of this cell and find that it does *not* fit the Requirem –

which it does not – we can make this entire part of the structure come crumbling down and escape!"

"And what are we going to use?" came the Red's next question. "Don't tell me you have a sledgehammer or a pickaxe in that displaced bag of yours."

"No, no…" Now it was Aldrin who grimaced. "I displaced those two and they never came back… I think the pickaxe is stuck up in the mountains somewhere…"

Zachtia shook her head. "So, what do we have?"

"These." Aldrin took a small bag that was not on him the last time Zachtia checked and opened it up.

When Zachtia looked inside, she could not mask the doubt in her voice. "Coins?"

"Well, yes, and my battle lance," Aldrin shrugged.

"Ugh." It did not help that her morning sickness had returned to haunt her. "Well, you two go on ahead calculating…I think I'll get more sleep." She scooted over to the door and put her back to it, closed her eyes…and Aldrin and Endia spoke more quietly to each other when they saw she had fallen asleep.

It was mid-morning when she woke up again; her morning sickness subsided fairly significantly. So had the bantering of her companions – now they just were sitting down, eating the breakfast of grits that the warden must have given them. "Could I have some?" she asked. "I'm starving."

A voice came from the other side of the door. "I thought as much."

With a startled gasp, Zachtia looked out the door and saw the warden squatting by it, holding another bowl of grits. "So…" he said. "Planning on escaping, are you?"

Aldrin shrugged, unconcerned. "Only if things go badly."

"What things go badly?" asked the warden.

"You could die," replied Aldrin.

"By whose hands?"

"The family that put us here in the first place." Aldrin stood up. "Sir, believe me when I say I fear for your life. I, for one, don't like being in here, but I don't want anyone else killed on my behalf."

The warden looked up at him. "Tell me…you're not one for revenge, *are* you?"

Aldrin blinked, unprepared for the question. "Those who do wrong will be brought to right through the law," he said more mechanically than he wished. "It's a war…I don't have any qualms with you."

"But you're our enemy," the male Red pointed out. "We've slaughtered your kind down to just you. It's really quite pitiable. I should just kill you now and end your lonely existence – but I won't. I guess that's just me being a Red – wanting to keep the last Green alive."

The warden pushed a bowl of grits to Zachtia and she caught it. "I can take care of myself," he said and started to walk back to his desk.

"And if you die?" called Aldrin.

"If I die, Green," the Red called back with a chuckle. "You have my permission to escape!"

As soon as Aldrin saw the warden sit down, he heard Endia call his name. "Yes, Endia?"

"Um…my father taught me probabilities when I was very young," Endia started uncomfortably. "The proper term for the process is *Qitnam-Lamathum*, and I've become quite good at it."

"Yes?" asked Zachtia a bit impatiently, wiping the bit of the meal slush that had sloshed onto her hand and the side of her dress. "Is this leading up to anything?"

"I've managed to make a *Qitnam-Lamathum* problem on his safety…by my calculations…" Her voice was shaking, "…we'll escape tonight."

Chapter 9

It was late afternoon before the preparations for escape were completed. To Zachtia's bemusement, Aldrin had carefully placed each coin where he had drawn an "X" and tapped it carefully with the butt of his shortened lance. He had repeated the process until he had 123 coins placed at 123 spots in the cell. She noticed that the warden had come to watch for some of the process and commented that it looked ridiculous…but he returned to his seat after a while, commenting that it was the oddest thing, seeing that the Green had a battle lance but was not using it to break the doors down. All of them were surprised but grateful that the warden actually let Aldrin keep the lance. Endia surmised that it was because Aldrin was not using it aggressively.

Finally, he took the 124th one and placed it in the center of the room. "When the time comes, we'll tap this one in the exact center of the room," he said softly. "That should destabilize the entire structure of the cell."

Zachtia shook her head. "Amazing. You sure it is going to work? Have you ever done this before?"

"Only once…" Aldrin trailed off. "Counting this time."

Endia giggled and Zachtia rolled her eyes. "Well, for your sake, I hope it works."

"For *all* our sakes, Zachtia," Aldrin said.

They all heard a tap on the bars on the cell door and turned to find that the warden was tapping one of the three bowls he was carrying. "Suppertime," he said, clearing his throat.

All of them walked over, thanked him for the meal, and sat down. Endia took time to smell the aroma of baked and semi-salted grits...and immediately set the bowl down. "Something's wrong!"

Aldrin almost had a spoonful to his mouth but immediately gave a sniff before it progressed any farther. "You're right... Zachtia –?"

The Red had already put hers down. "Not touching it," she said warily.

The warden was still at the door. "What's wrong?" he asked nervously. "I didn't touch it – it comes to my jail via ration delivery...I just serve it."

(Here Aldrin noticed that the man looked flushed, but not in anger...and his breathing sounded raspy.)

Endia explained, "We Yellow elves know how to differentiate smells. These grits don't smell like grits."

Aldrin took another, long sniff. "I'm not sure...no...I am sure." He pushed the grits bowl farther away from him. "It's been poisoned with Dalakara extract. The stuff kills in about an hour after ingestion."

Zachtia looked at the warden in shock and anger. "You tried to *poison* us?"

But the warden had slumped into a sitting position. "Poisoned..."

"Warden?" Aldrin rushed over. "Warden, what's wrong – tell me."

"I...I always eat the grits when I'm here," said the warden. "Heh...it's a habit..."

Aldrin's eyes widened and Endia gasped. "How long ago did you have supper?" the Green asked.

The warden swallowed and it looked like it took a lot of effort to do so. "...half an hour ago."

Aldrin let out a puff of air. "There might be time – I don't know." He examined the elf's dilated pupils and listened to the elf's breathing and heartbeat. He shook his head. "I really don't know...I'll do whatever I can."

The elf's breath was heavier now. "I think not."

"No!" Zachtia cried. "Aldrin can help you! Aldrin, don't you have a cure?"

"I have something that can be mixed with water and it can clear it up – but I did it within minutes of contamination!" Aldrin said frustratedly. "But there's still a *chance*. Warden, you've got to let me help."

"Green...Aldrin." Another breath, heavier than the first, "It's too late. I'm an old elf and have done my time..." Another ragged breath, as if, now aware it was dying, his body decided to just get it over with. "...listen to me."

The warden pulled Aldrin closer to him, almost putting Aldrin's face into the bars. "Those who poisoned me..." his draw of breath raked through his lungs. "...will be back. I'm sure ...it's the friends you made at the tavern."

Aldrin grimaced. "It's my fault, then?"

The elf tried to derisively chuckle but it came out gurgled. His voice was at a hoarse whisper. "Every elf ...is responsible for his own actions. You did the right thing, Aldrin. You're just in here because you're a Green, isn't it? Escape … help Zachtia find Dairlo…and tell him…"

Aldrin grasped the man's hand and gave it a shake. "Tell him what? Tell him *what,* warden?"

The elf took one last breath and it sounded as though he was breathing water, "…that Commander Aleborn wishes him a long…life…"

With that, the elf went limp…and his eyes darkened.

Aldrin bit his lip as he gazed upon the warden/commander's body. "Aleborn," he said. "…Commander Aleborn led the Battle of Redblood. He was the first one to call a retreat when we were winning. This must have been his punishment for retreating." The Green sighed and stood up. "Right…let's carry out his last wishes. Let's escape."

Immediately Endia was at the cell doors. "I can't see his keys!" she said. It was not until she looked up that she said, "Oh…how convenient. They're on his desk."

"Back to the original plan, then," Aldrin said firmly.

Both of them nodded and walked back to him. "Alright," he said firmly, "You know your designated areas to stand."

"Right," Endia said quickly. "I'll stand at designated brick 12x23, while Zachtia –"

"Stands in the corner – no designations, thank you," said Zachtia.

Aldrin cleared his throat. "Right, you'll stand in the corner. Both of you, get into position now."

A Warrior's Code

As soon as they got into position, Aldrin went to the far wall and picked up the lance where he had left it. He went back to position and got ready to hammer his lance straight down onto the vertical coin…but then craned his head so his left ear was in the air. "What's that?"

Zachtia began, "Are we now jumping at noi –"

Endia cut her off. "Shh…I hear it too…it sounds like a wheelbarrow."

An utterly familiar male voice rang out, "Quite correct, Yellow!"

Aldrin immediately went to the bars. "Oh, no," he whispered.

It was the noble. What was worse, Aldrin could see five others in his wake, perhaps eight. The wheelbarrow that they were hearing was being pushed by the noble and was stacked with hay and wood. Lastly, one of the noble's henchmen carried a torch.

Aldrin had already figured out what was going to happen. "This is insane, Red. Why on earth would you-?"

"Why? Because you didn't die from the poison!" laughed the noble. "No, seriously, the reasons are quite simple…I was beaten by a Green and I-I can't accept that. So, I'm taking you out along with all the rest of the useless clutter."

He walked over to the cell that held the three and looked down at the commander-turned-warden. He made a face. "Pity," he said. "I wanted to kill him myself, disrespecting me like that. Oh well."

"You did with the poison," Aldrin said. "Does that make you feel any better?"

"Oh! See, I thought you had killed him. Easiest thing in the world, kill him – the dog was so old."

Aldrin made a grab for him and he scampered out of the way like the weasel he was. As soon as he was out of reach, he squinted through the bars. "Are those coins?"

"Yes," replied Aldrin evenly.

"You're sticking coins into the wall?"

"Yes."

"You're sticking coins in the wall for *what* purpose?" came the next question.

"If you must know, it's to escape," Aldrin said, seeing an opportunity. "But, if you open that door, there will be no need, now would there?"

It looked as if the noble was considering it. But then he smirked and said, "No…no-no-no, I see what you're trying to do – and it *won't* work, Green. It *won't!*" The noble walked back to his group and grabbed the torch from his henchman's hand. "Try your little escape plan. There are scant windows in here – I suspect you'll be unconscious in five minutes, give-or-take, and dead in seven. Not being able to breathe is so unpleasant."

The noble chuckled sadistically. "Have fun escaping!" he said, and dropped the torch into the thick of the hay and wood.

Aldrin raced back to the center of the room as the fire scampered across the bramble. "We need to do this and we need to do it *now!*" he barked.

He picked up his lance, turned the coin vertically once again, and slammed the lance into it for all his worth.

Instantly the floor cracked from the coin to the far wall, spider-webbing across the far wall, carried over to the front wall…and stopped.

Aldrin was horrified as he raced to the where the wall was cracked. He slammed the business end of his lance into a loose piece and gave a twist, knocking it out of the wall. "That's not good," he said.

The wall had been reinforced with tubes of metal. The metal had rusted over but it was holding steady.

"Aldrin!" Zachtia cried when she saw the problem, "What do we – *cough* – do?"

Endia called out, "We can't move the coins! Not enough time!"

The sound of the flames was getting stronger as well as the smoke. Aldrin could barely keep himself from coughing as he stepped back from the wall. "Okay, uh the Immaculate Disposition ratified by the obtuse triangle equalized by Rae's Polygon Requirem…" he said out loud to keep his head clear as he calculated. "Carry the seven, drop the eight…*got it*."

"*Cough, cough* Aldrin! What are you…?" Zachtia was fading, her eyes drooping.

Endia called out, "Aldrin, she's going to pass out!"

Aldrin quickly twisted his lance so it came apart into two clubs and tossed Endia one of them. "Endia! Go to coin 13-by-47 Hurry!"

She staggered over to the coin she knew was 13-by-47. "I'm here!"

"Hit it! Now!" Aldrin slammed the coin he was standing before with the butt of his club while Endia did the same with her coin.

The crack started up once again, this time from the two places! Soon it was at the ceiling and Aldrin and Endia raced back to Zachtia who had passed out in the middle of the room. Aldrin put the pieces of his lance back together. "Stay close!" he said to Endia.

Her arms grappled around him as the ceiling began to crumble. Chunks of it began to fall at random and Aldrin had to react quickly as some almost crushed them. He wrenched his lance left and right, back and forth to block the pieces from hitting the group, some slamming into his shoulders and arms before falling away.

The entire cell structure came apart, revealing the rusted metal piping that ran through it and vertically up and over back to the main structure.

Soon, Aldrin, Endia, and Zachtia were sitting in a cloud of dust and smoke. Aldrin, bloodied and bruised, looked down at the two female elves, breathing thanks that they were unharmed…but soon was growling savagely as he heard the voices of the noble and his gang shouting out in confusion. *"Let's end this,"* he muttered.

With the strength provided by the adrenalin and fury for all that had happened pumping through his veins, he hoisted Zachtia in his arms, rushed to the bars that had daylight running through them through the smog, and slammed his foot into one of the bars, then the next, cracking them and breaking them in another round of kicks. "With me, Endia."

Endia had trouble keeping up as he rushed through the smoke and dust, but spotted him clearly as they broke into the sunlight.

She spotted the men, eight of them, running to them. "They're carrying weapons!" she called to Aldrin.

"Who cares," he replied. He walked over to a little tree with grass around it and set Zachtia under the tree. "I have you to back me up." His eyes darted to a strong branch of the tree. He broke it off with a bit of effort and handed it to her. "Your weapon."

With that, they rushed toward the group, which was surprised with the offense.

Immediately the Yellow and Green were in the midst of the men and the battle began. Aldrin focused on two elves with swords. He met one's sword coming down and parried the other's with a swing of the other end of his staff. He pulled back, catching the other elf's chin and forced his staff forward, forcing the elf in front of him to block.

A third elf came running into the mix, swinging a club! Aldrin took his lance and swung his entire body around, letting the weapon slide through his hands until he caught the far end of it.

The blow made all three of them stagger and Aldrin swung his lance up in another spin, slamming the third elf in the head, the first one in the waist, and the second in the legs. He instantly was behind the third elf and punched him in the middle of the back. With a cry of pain, the third elf was out of the fight. The other two came at him weakly, and he put the lance between them and swung low, tripping them both. With a vertical spin, he put both of them out of commission with blows to the head.

He turned to help Endia, who was holding her own quite well with the other five but getting tired and weak from smoke inhalation. Aldrin ran into the fray and took on three of them, slamming his lance into the middle one's chest then up into his chin, knocking him flat on the ground, unconscious.

The other two came at him with knives, slashing menacingly. He caught one's hand with his staff and turned it up, but not before it had sliced into his bicep. In a cry of pain and fury, he wrenched the elf's arm around so he heard a crack of bone then down came the lance onto the elf's head, instantly rendering him unconscious.

The remaining elf was taken down by a blow to his head. Aldrin turned his attention to Endia to find that she had put hers out of commission also and was now pointing. *"Look!* It's the noble!"

Aldrin whipped his head around to find that the noble was running as fast as he could from the jail and immediately whipped his lance around to throw it like a javelin…

Except he did not throw it. "No…" he whispered. He lowered his arm which was now shaking.

"No? He's responsible! He-" cried Endia, confused.

"He can do no more," Aldrin said softly. "His friends are gone and he has been beaten once again." He looked at the Yellow. Other than a few cuts to her face and shoulder and a torn dress, she looked well. He looked at the smoldering remains of the prison. "We need to get cleaned up and our wounds dressed. Let's go back to Zachtia. We'll discuss what to do next afterward."

Chapter 10

Zachtia slowly roused to the sunlight streaming through the leaves of the trees in the distance, she herself looking around at the blurred faces of her comrades. "We're...still alive?" she asked, sitting up.

Aldrin walked over and knelt beside her. "Surprisingly," he said softly. Zachtia could see he was still shaking from the fallout of the adrenaline rush and, in this position, he was fighting to keep his balance, albeit slightly. His arm was bandaged and he was holding it at a tender position at his side. He was still a bit musty – so was she, she realized to her disdain – but she saw Endia behind him washing off with the water from a large pitcher. "I'm next with that," she called to the elf.

Endia, finishing up, brought the pitcher over with a cloth towel that was large enough she could have used it as a blanket. "I'm glad you're okay," she said, smiling at the Red elf.

Aldrin grinned a little then glanced down at Zachtia's personal globe. "How is the baby?" he asked.

Zachtia focused on the life inside her as she got to her knees and splashed the cool water on her arms. The little life was unharmed, thanks to Aldrin's heroics, but Zachtia sensed its confusion. "...a bit confused," she said finally. "But unhurt." She continued to clean off, using both hands to splash water on her face. "So, what have I missed?" she asked, coming up for air and gesturing for the towel.

Aldrin took the pitcher and began cleaning himself off while he spoke. "When the dust settled, I went back to the jail to see if I could find anything. I was able to dig up most of our confiscated supplies, and I found out that there were three other prisoners that were mildly hurt in the collapsing of our cell."

"I attended to the prisoners," Endia continued. "They said they were all there because they ruffled the noble's feathers."

"I don't doubt it," huffed Zachtia, her voice muffled by the towel.

Aldrin motioned for the towel and continued, "They said they caught most of what happened and said they more or less believed my story, enough to keep our involvement with this incident under wraps."

Zachtia nodded slowly. "Good." She felt a little better, now that her face and arms were clean. She couldn't wait for a proper bath.

Aldrin helped her to her feet and she looked at him. "So, where do we go from here?" she asked, waving him off gently after steadying herself.

The Green looked to the east. Zachtia could see his face furrowing in concentration. "Scarlesh is in that direction," he said, pointing to the horizon and the rising sun. "To reach it, we will have to pass through the Wanderer's Bane. It's a series of deep, maze-like canyons; from what I've heard, the entire stretch of them is about eight miles across. If all goes well, we'll reach the canyons within two days and get to the other side in another three, maybe four. Then we'll get to a thick forest which is about a mile across…then it's a straight shot to the city."

Zachtia listened to this timeline with both hope and caution. His last prediction on how long it would take to get to Scarlesh was a week and it had taken three to reach the Yellow encampment, and two more to travel from there to here. But she was quietly optimistic, now that they had experienced a brush with death close to what her husband had gone through when he was out with the troops, and had survived. The more she thought about him the more excited and wistful she got...

Aldrin gritted his teeth as he looked at the horizon. What he had refrained from telling Zachtia was that the Wanderer's Bane had not been given its name for no reason. It was a geographical defense of Scarlesh in that there was no single, straight path leading through it. At best, it was a dizzying labyrinth of close walls, winding passages, and narrow ravines, all winding around, though, and within each other. At worst, it was a tomb. What Aldrin had also kept to himself was the fact that these canyons, due to their treacherous nature and their habit of entrapping unsuspecting travelers, were said to be haunted by thieves and bandit gangs. *"If all goes well,"* Aldrin heard himself repeating under his breath. He hoped he wouldn't end up eating those words. He had memorized the shortest distance between the in and the out, but this would be the first time he had to actually *navigate* Wanderer's Bane.

As he turned to put out the small campfire he had made the night before, he heard Endia's cheerful voice say, "We're almost there! Come on, let's get started!"

They were within half a mile of the cliffs of the Wanderer's Bane and they could clearly see them. Endia gave a whistle in awe of the sheer magnitude of the cliffs, menacingly blocking their path.

"Just like it was described…" she said. "I don't think you want me to tell you the odds."

"Um, no," came Zachtia's prompt reply.

The road they were on dipped in a slope that had to be navigated slowly, Aldrin many times being the focal point and ground for the two lady elves as they scraped and tracked down the slope. This slope continued for about half an hour more of travel, the cliffs now looking like the Council-City skyscrapers, light showing through the gaps of the cliffs.

They walked cautiously but quickly. Endia always had her child-like fascination…but now she was apprehensively taking in the sights. She knew full well what could lurk in the darkness and the shadows. She so much, though, wanted to examine some of the rock to determine why it lightly sparkled.

Zachtia's excitement had dimmed significantly as she too watched. She did not know fully of the dangers of Wanderer's Bane, but she was always watching for that occasional falling rock that had finally come loose from its foundation, or listening attentively as the echoes of small rock slides came from in front of them. She followed closely behind Aldrin, gritting her teeth and flinching each time she heard a disturbance.

Of all of them, Aldrin was the most prepared and the most concerned. He did not jump or even flinch at sounds like Zachtia, nor did he look around in fear like Endia. He did though note all the disturbances sounding around him, calculating their distance, and he was always using his peripheral vision to look about himself. His lance was in its shortened form in his right hand, ready to be opened if necessary. He was relying on the instructions he memorized when in his division…he hoped he remembered it all correctly.

The minutes dragged on, the hours seeming like days. Were it not for Endia's precise calculations, they would have lost all track of time. They rested, ate, walked for hours, rested, ate, and walked for more hours.

Everyone's morale started to sag during the second hour of the second day they were in the labyrinth…would it never end? Aldrin's already shaky confidence with his internal map was waning, too. He would spend at least ten minutes of each hour standing in the middle of the small path, his eyes closed, feeling the sunlight hitting him and making calculations in his head.

It was on the third day that something finally broke through the monotony:

Endia was trying to get everyone to sing a song with her and having no luck, when Aldrin stopped everyone and craned his left ear up. "Sh-shh…I hear something…"

The two ladies froze and both followed Aldrin's example. "What is it?" asked Endia.

Zachtia was listening intently. "…another rock slide?"

"No, no…listen a little longer," said Aldrin. "Rock-slide, yes, but a lot of little ones…and the way they're spaced apart – someone's on the cliffs above us!"

No sooner had he finished his sentence but a shout was heard overhead! Aldrin looked up just in time to see a dart fly down and imbed itself into his shoulder. Darkness clouded his vision as he stumbled towards Zachtia and Endia, but both of them had already fallen.

It was all he could do to put his lance into his pocket and displace it...and the last thing he saw before he succumbed to the darkness was what looked like half a swarm of shadows flying down ropes from the cliff tops.

Aldrin came to and he felt someone digging around in his left pant pocket. "This Green sure travels light," he heard a male's voice mutter.

Aldrin said softly, "You'd be surprised," and heard his assailant stand up in a hurry.

Aldrin opened his eyes. They were in a clearing and it was nighttime, a fire blazed in the middle of the clearing, being made up of the withered trees one would occasionally see clinging to the rocks and frozen in their quest to seek sunshine. There were about twelve of the figures – not half the swarm that Aldrin falsely saw while his head was swimming – and they were all dressed in black; some in rags, others in suits fit for assassins, complete with belt and hood.

Zachtia and Endia were both unconscious and at the far end of the cave. Aldrin could see that they were unharmed, but bound.

He tested the bonds that were binding his own arms behind him. Pretty strong.

He looked up at his assailant. He judged him to be about 400 years old, stark white hair and an equally white, trimmed beard. His eyes were sharp, looking at Aldrin with a keenness that ebbed intelligence. His expression was cool and calm -- not with the arrogance of the Red noble, but with a Green's confidence and wisdom. He was dressed in an assassin's suit: black pants and dragon-scale chainmail behind a black tank top. A cloak that would usually shroud the shoulders and head was now worn as a cape, the hood resting across the shoulders and back. His boots were leather, but the bottoms of them had a gummy substance that Aldrin concluded helped him scale the rock face.

All-in-all, he looked as if he had been playing hunter for a long time.

Aldrin finally decided an ambassadorial approach was called for. "Greetings," he said. "I would shake your hand but mine seem to be tied up, sorry."

The elder broke into a small smile. "They won't be for long -- I just didn't know if you were going to be civil." His voice was deep and smooth, like a lake in a deep cavern. "Around here my men call me Hunter. How about you, Green?"

"I guess 'Gatherer' is out of the question, eh?" Aldrin straightened a little. "My name is Aldrin, last of the Green Elves, save on the Council of Four. So tell me...why are you here, and what is with the black color? I haven't had any information that there was a 'Black Tribe' in the mix."

"Interesting question from a Gatherer, Aldrin," said Hunter, starting to walk a slow arc around the Green. "But I'll answer: in the war, my men were like yourselves. There were Reds and Yellows, and there may have been a Green or two."

That made Aldrin's full attention swing to Hunter's words. Greens? Might he not be the last one?

Hunter went on, "One by one, they wandered into the Bane and sooner or later got lost. Then I found them, nursed many of them back to health, and became their leader. They chose to forego their 'color codes' and become the beautiful, void color, Black."

Aldrin nodded slowly. "I understand...except for one thing: your origins."

A Warrior's Code

This time the Black elf grinned in an unsettling, mysterious way. "Wouldn't you like to know?"

Aldrin nodded. "Yes, I would! Just one question then -- answer me this: were you a Green elf?"

The Black elf crouched down and motioned for Aldrin to turn and loosened the bonds when Aldrin did so. He whispered in Aldrin's ear, "I will give you one simple clue and I bet...I really bet you can tell me what "color code" I was from yourself."

Aldrin rubbed his wrists. "What's the bet?"

Hunter stood up. "The bet is," the Black elf said, "You and your friend's lives. If you guess right, I will send one of my men with you to give you safe passage through the Wanderer's Bane. If you don't, well...my men haven't had a good meal in days."

Aldrin nearly gagged. "That's...a repulsive thought. I accept on those terms. What is your clue?"

Hunter began walking away and said over his shoulder, "I just gave it to you, Aldrin. You have one hour."

"He's a Red..." Endia said quietly. "...he's gotta be."

By the middle of the hour given, both ladies had awakened and were talking with Aldrin. Hunter had given him permission to discuss it with them as long as it was Aldrin who gave the answer.

"What's the alternative, Aldrin?" asked Zachtia. "He's not short, so he's definitely not a Yellow, you're absolutely sure that he's not a Green from the response he gave you...so he's gotta be a cannibalistic Red!"

"You left a tribe out. Zachtia," Aldrin said softly.

"Well obviously!" exclaimed the Red. "He couldn't possibly be a Purple! One, they look more like demons than elves, and two, they're utterly and completely animalistic!"

"Which has got me thinking...no." Aldrin looked at Hunter who was by the fire. "It can't be."

"We agree then!" Zachtia started to say, but trailed off when Aldrin held up a hand.

"But all the clues fit...but that's just a legend...oh but if it could be true..."

"Aldrin!" both lady elves said and Aldrin snapped out of it. "I've been on the road for a long time. In the beginning of my trek -- basically to get my head out of the mud of depression -- I went to the City of the Council where I went to the Four Tower Library. I immersed myself into the reading of basically everything, and I stumbled upon a history book that contained the origins of --"

"As the moon reads, Aldrin," Hunter said, "You have about twenty minutes."

Aldrin got up and faced Hunter. "I not only know who you are, but I also know why you so easily came to be the leader of these elves."

Hunter looked impressed. "Really? Please, explain it in the usual Green fashion so that your companions can be filled in."

"Long ago," Aldrin said, "During the time of Peace, there were four tribes: Red, Yellow, Green, and Blue tribes. They each had a different 'Tribal Attribute'. The Blue tribe was not only one of the most wise and knowledgeable tribes, they also had one thing they could do that the other tribes couldn't: expel their energies as physical light beams. As they learned to use this power, the energy soon 'carved' designs into their bodies, the designs glowing whenever the power was used. Now, the ancient Blue Tribe thought it was magic, so they studied the designs and duplicated them into mystical carvings in circles and octagons, using their knowledge of math. Soon, they even "deciphered" a language out of the markings and began making chants.

"For a time, these worked and they began getting stronger and stronger...but the other tribes saw the Blue Tribe was also getting more animalistic. Soon, at one dark ceremony, a large group of Blues tore apart six Yellow children as a sacrifice to the Markings and ate the Yellows while drawing the markings on the ground and singing the markings in their "deciphered" language.

"Suddenly the group's own skin tone began to change -- and they weren't the only ones! All the Blues across the land began changing. Their bodies mutated, becoming like demon spawn, and their skin darkened and colored into what we know as purple."

Aldrin took a step towards Hunter. "Impossibly, I call you out as a Purple, but maybe more accurately a Blue elf, feeding energy to the lost of Wanderer's Bane and gaining their loyalty. What say you?"

Hunter was silent, looking at the three. Then a primeval growl quietly emitted from his throat before he turned it into a sigh. He finally smiled and said, "Very…very good, Aldrin. I'm…I'm not surprised you figured me out."

"Look at your knuckles," Aldrin said quietly.

Both Zachtia and Endia involuntarily looked at the knuckles of the Blue elf and saw little rivulets of light just starting to glow on them; small designs that looked like ancient hieroglyphics but more twisted and exotic.

Hunter brought his hands up, gazing at them. "Yes. It is time."

"Time for what?" asked Endia.

Instead of answering her, Hunter walked to where he was near the fire, and called out, "My men! ...my brothers, come to me."

The twelve – Aldrin could count them now, exactly twelve – men gathered together around the fire and looked expectantly at Hunter. To Aldrin, they looked like a pack of hungry wolves around the leader's kill.

Hunter continued, "My brothers, it is now time for all of you to feed...and a sacrifice to be made. This full moon did not bring us the pleasure of feeding on new light, so one of our own must provide for his brothers. I say to you again, whoever does it, that you will join the brothers who have made the sacrifice in the past. Your memory will never die and you will never be gone, for you will be with us and within us."

The pack of men looked at each other, wonder and contemplation on their faces.

Aldrin held his breath and Zachtia whispered to him, "Ugh, I don't think I want to see this."

Endia had already curled herself tightly onto Aldrin's arm, her face planted at the middle of his upper arm, one eye open to the horror that was about to commence.

Finally, one of the black elves, a middle-aged elf with dark skin and stocky physique, raised his hand and said, "I'll do it…for the good of all."

Knowing what came next, the rest of the elves except for Hunter took two steps back from the fire and went to one knee. The firelight blazed, making the shadows dance and gave sinister, savage light upon Hunter and the kneeling Black elf. Hunter nodded. "Thank you, my brother. May you always be *remembered…*"

Suddenly his own physique changed! His teeth grew in his mouth and his jaw dropped, his eyes glowed a bright white as his mouth opened in an ear-splitting, gut wrenching howl! His muscles rippled as his markings blasted light out from his clothing. He pointed at the elf with a long, clawed finger and what looked like liquid lightning blasted from it and hit the elf square in the chest. The elf in turn spasmed as his own skin momentarily brightened with the markings…and then disappeared into light altogether.

The resulting energy cascaded in a wave and separated into twelve shares, each gliding through the air and passing into the remaining black elves, Hunter included.

Hunter fell to his knees, breathing heavily. His body shrank back, his face and hands returned to normal. He slowly felt his face, grounding this fact in his mind, and slowly stood up. "Thank you, my brother," he whispered. "May you always be remembered."

Aldrin realized he had been holding his breath and breathed in and out a couple of times. As his senses recovered from the shock, he noticed that Endia was whimpering…and Zachtia had once again passed out.

Chapter 11

Aldrin was not surprised that Zachtia's waking words were, "Okay, Aldrin, explain *that* to me."

Aldrin was sitting next to her and had been pondering the events that had occurred for about half an hour. "Well..." he said slowly, "we can rule out magic because that's what reverts Blues to Purples. What is logical to assume is that his Blue elf form is only temporary and has to be sustained by periodical 'feeding' on another elf's energy. This would then lead to a possibility: he finds the lost of Wander's Bane and heals them with his energy – everything is made up and powered by some type of energy, if I am to understand it in my reading of Blue theory...so he could very well have found a way to speed up an elf's natural healing via powering it...I'm not sure. Whether he did or not, he gained their loyalty as well as gave himself not only a food supply, but a way to stay a Blue elf. That's my explanation – giving the others energy is just another way of gaining their loyalty and keeping them fed."

Zachtia almost gagged and Endia breathed out slowly. "That's...such a horrid way to live," the Yellow whispered.

They heard Hunter's deep voice, "But it is a way, Yellow."

They all turned and Hunter smiled a little as he tapped his left ear. "Blue hearing. I can hear an army of ants marching across the ground here – sounds like the war." He walked over to them and sat down, Aldrin at his left, Zachtia in front of him, Endia next to her. "I gave you my word I would grant you safe passage through Wander's Bane," he said. "I intend to uphold that promise. I tell you though, Aldrin, Zachtia, Endia, that you will not be given such privilege on our next meeting." He sighed. "No one is coming into the Bane anymore," he said softly, folding his hands in a pyramid fashion near his face. "I am running out of men. I used to have dozens, both men and women…down to eleven."

"Because you consumed them," Endia said, her eyes narrowing.

"How would *you* go on, Endia?" snapped Hunter fiercely. "How would you go, day by day, knowing that if you didn't consume the life energy of one elf – *one elf* – every two weeks that you would devolve into an animal that had no other inclination but to ravage dozens more each day?" He breathed out in a sigh. "I am the last of my race, as far as I can see. Hm…last of the Blue elves."

Aldrin bit his lip. "…I can relate."

Hunter looked at him with those sharp, intelligent eyes. "Why do you think I'm letting you go? I was there in the group when they captured you all. You all looked so…out of place – I almost thought the war was over, seeing you all, practically hand-in-hand. Finally, I pieced together why you all were travelling together and I decided to give you a chance – I just needed something to test you."

Endia's head went up. "Oh! That's why you gave Aldrin that clue – when you told him you and your men would eat him if he didn't guess right."

"I knew Aldrin would cancel his own color out immediately…but I wasn't sure if he knew the origins of the Purple elves – speaking of which…"

Hunter leaned in closer. "You have a tracker on your scent. My men have been watching a Purple elf coming the same way you were. We have tried the sleeper darts on him but it just made him angrier. I've told my men to stay back – it is *your* problem, not ours. We can easily hide in the darkness."

"Excuse me," Zachtia said with a tempered voice, "but did you not say you would grant us safe passage through Wanderer's Bane? I hardly call being chased by a Purple safe."

Hunter nodded. "Right you are, and we will provide that safe passage through the Goblyn mine tunnels *under* Wanderer's Bane. But I have a pretty good idea that the Purple will find a way out of the Bane and then will be right back to tracking you in the Barrier Forest of Scarlesh. That is where you will have to face him."

Aldrin's eyebrows went up. "The *Goblyn* mines? Weren't the Goblyns an ancient race?"

Hunter's eyebrows went up also. "Very good, Aldrin. Yes, they were – some ways more advanced than us Blues in the times of old – and it is said that they were expert trappers and miners."

"Anything else we should know?" asked Zachtia, leaning forward.

Hunter looked at her. "A Red is asking for more information?"

Zachtia threw her hands up, "So I'm starting to see the advantages of it, blame him!" she jerked her finger at Aldrin who managed to grin apologetically and elicit a giggle from Endia.

"Well if you must know," said Hunter, having the slightest hint of amusement on his face, "They were also said to have been able to channel natural magic, like the Blue's energy, but more importantly they were able to tell the future."

Endia perked up. "How did they do that?"

"No one knows," said Hunter dismissively. "Or do we? You'll have to find out – I grow tired of this."

Hunter stood up and called over one of his men; a slimmer but more agile fellow with slanted eyes and dark red hair. "This young man has been with me for quite a long while," Hunter said proudly. "We have both owed each other our lives and paid the debt countless times. He is familiar with the Goblyn Mines. He'll be the one to lead you safely through."

The young man looked at them. "Call me Dalian."

Zachtia saw Aldrin give him a strange look. "Dalian…good to meet you," he said finally.

"Well!" said Zachtia, "When are we going?"

They left early the next morning. Aldrin had suggested it, seeing that since they were going through ancient mines, they would have little light as-is. He thought that their best option was to get going as soon as the sun started peeking over the horizon.

Zachtia was glad to be getting out of that environment – the ambiance sent chills down her spine, especially since she kept getting mental images of the feeding ceremony. She shuddered once again and turned back to their guide who was making preparations for the journey. By now, he had changed into a more rugged uniform of black; the same boots as Hunter, gauntlets, a crossbow hanging on his belt, little packs filled with supplies accompanying the crossbow. Again, Zachtia caught Aldrin looking at him with a very curious expression – one that flowed with what she could only decipher as wonder and a little bit of apprehension. She walked over to him (Endia in tow) and asked softly, "What's up? You look like you've seen a ghost."

A Warrior's Code

Aldrin looked at her. "Perhaps I have," he said. "'Dalian' was one of the names on the active-duty roster when I was a cadet in the Bacht. He was said to be one of the clever Greens in the squadron – and he was said to be the most paranoid, too. I never met him and never had the chance to – he and his scout group went missing and were never found – and here's the thing that disturbs me most of all: they went looking for a more defensive position and their last report said something about finding *mines*."

Zachtia gasped softly. "Do you think this is Dalian? *The* Dalian?"

"I'm certainly not ruling it out," said Aldrin quietly. "It could be him or one of his descendants – we did have women Greens in our squadrons. They seemed to know a lot more on how to communicate and had a sense of direction that helped greatly."

"Incredible," Zachtia breathed. "About Dalian. I understand the 'women intuition' thing."

Aldrin made a face at her and Endia came up closer to them. "I think we're ready to leave," she said quietly. "While you two were talking, Dalian went over to Hunter and they are now talking."

When Zachtia and Aldrin turned and looked, they caught the remains of a mutual shoulder-grasp as Dalian and Hunter said goodbye, then Dalian walked back over to the group. "Are you all ready to go?" he asked.

Zachtia could see Aldrin trying hard to hold back his questions so she answered first, "Yes, we're ready Dalian – more than ready, actually."

Once again, Aldrin found himself navigating the Bane, except he was not the only one doing the navigation, more the lead. Dalian kept a good distance in front of the three elves, but kept in sight, looking back like Aldrin did. Aldrin had opted to carry their supplies while Dalian carried any necessary food, both items stored in burlap sacks and slung securely over the shoulders as backpacks...

Dalian...

The name kept repeating in the Green's head, the image of the roster flashing across his mind's eye. Perhaps the only other Green in existence.

Except on the Council of Four, he reminded himself. Still, he hardly counted them: they all lived in the City of the Council and guarded it. They said they guarded the outside tribes too...but since the enmity between the tribes began, the Council became more reclusive, never poking their collective heads out of the Council Tower for any given reason.

So, he was somewhat right in calling himself the last of the Green elves. He did not truly know if the Green Elf -- or elves, he was not sure how many -- was still alive, or even if the Reds had assassinated the Green Council member.

He shook himself out of his thoughts and brought his focus back to Dalian. The Black elf was standing on a rock cliff face and was waiting expectantly. Aldrin waited for Zachtia and Endia to catch up with him and then they all went up the cliff face. Dalian pointed downwards, and all three elves looked down.

There, below them, was a massive cavern entranceway. It was a gaping hole and the only way down into it was a stairway chiseled directly into the rock face itself.

"Our way down," Dalian said after the elves had taken it all in. "It's three straight days through the mines."

Endia waved her hand and Dalian bemusedly said, "Yes, Endia?"

"Did you account for the speed that a pregnant elf walks?" she asked. "Or the times that we'll have to eat and sleep?"

"Yes I did, little one," said Dalian quietly. "If it were not for those factors we'd be in and out within a day, maybe even half a day. But because we'll have to eat and sleep *and* contend with a pregnant elf, it's three days at best. Understood?"

Endia's jaw went slack. "Uh...yep. Seems you're good at conjectural math! Ever read H'Raia's *Black Numbers*?"

This time Zachtia interrupted, "Could we get a move on?!"

Aldrin tried to swallow his chuckle and it turned into a cough, "Ah, yes, let's."

"Very well," Dalian said, turned, and began walking down the long stairs. Aldrin ushered the two ladies in front of him and he went last, looking up at the clouds once more before plunging himself into the darkness.

Darkness! It was almost tangible; thick, black darkness that momentarily blinded him as he practically stumbled down the stairs.

Zachtia's voice was heard, "I can't see a thing!"

"Your eyes will adjust," he heard Dalian say from a ways in front of them. "In the meantime, just put one foot in front of the other with the knowledge there's a hundred steps to the bottom."

Zachtia groaned and Endia's voice sounded off, "Could this be one of the Goblyn's ways of keeping out strangers? If one of us slips, the odds of that one making it down the stairs alive is...well, extremely low."

"Yes, which is why we must keep our feet," Dalian replied, "and if one must fall, then he will want to fall backwards."

Aldrin did not like to think of falling either way. He focused on the steps, how they felt under his booted feet. He kind of wished he had switched his boots out for his forest buffalo-skin shoes. They were much more flexible and even though they protected the feet from anything sharp short of a sword, they certainly allowed the feet to feel the presence of such an object.

Downward they all trekked. It was about five minutes before Dalian finally said, "Found the bottom, be ready."

Maybe he was a Red, Aldrin mused. *He certainly knows how to get to the point.*

Soon enough, he heard Endia and Zachtia proclaim their discovery of the base of the steps and a few seconds afterward he himself was walking on flat ground instead of step. By this time, his vision had grown accustomed to the darkness, but it was such complete blackness he could only see what the reflected light from the steps showed, mainly the forms of his companions.

The tallest one -- Dalian -- said to him, "Aldrin, now would be a good time to reach into that supplies bag and pull out a Lumen Crystal."

Aldrin was an expert at fishing out items in the dark -- he had to, having most of his supplies displaced in a bag on his shoulders. He took off the backpack of supplies and fished around in it until he found a foot-size crystal that had been carefully carved into a six-point star shape. "Here you go," he said as he handed the crystal to the Black Elf.

The elf took it and walked to the group's left, disappearing in the shadows. After a few moments, however, they heard stone scrape across stone and the Lumen crystal glowed like a star in the night sky.

What it illuminated was a tunnel that was just high enough that they didn't hit their heads on the ceiling and wide enough they could have all stretched out their arms full length and stand finger-to-finger with no room to spare. The walls were also lined with black crystals of all shapes and sizes that glistened in the light.

Endia gave a low gasp in awe and even Zachtia looked impressed. "Wow, so, what's with all the black rocks?" asked the Red elf.

Dalian scoffed, "Watch your language, Miss Red. These are *onyx* stones mixed with Mica crystals."

"Onyx..." Aldrin echoed under his breath and suddenly all eyes were on him. He cleared his throat and said, "Something I read in the mythology section in the Four Towers Library. According to mythos, onyx stone...ugh." He scratched his head as if it would help. "It was written in some strange language that I was able to decipher a little bit of. It said something about 'time reflection' or something to that effect. Definitely time, as in the linear cause-to-effect to which we are bound, and then something like 'mirror' -- *reflection* being the best word in the context."

"So...what," Zachtia mused, "It said that onyx could reflect time?"

"Basically."

Endia had walked over to one of the larger stones on the wall to the right of them and was examining herself in it. "Goodness, I need a bath," she whispered. She said to the others, "I can't see the future, or the reflection of the future, for that matter."

Dalian walked over to her. "It could be just legend. Then again..." His eyebrows went up as he looked at her. "Maybe you are looking into a Mica. Stand back..." When she only took a step backward, he gestured, "Farther, all of you, against the wall away from this stone."

All of them hesitantly went to the left wall and Dalian went to the side of the stone, flattened himself against the wall beside it...and plucked the stone from the wall.

What happened next occurred in a split second: from the spot he had plucked the stone, a spear shot out and imbedded itself in the far wall.

Aldrin felt like his heart had jumped into his throat and both lady elves shrieked.

Dalian had tensed up, but then relaxed, tossed the stone up and caught it. "Yep, it was Mica."

Zachtia was immediately irked. "Don't *do* that!" she said roughly.

Dalian smirked and tossed the stone up again. "So...what have we learned?"

"Our guide wants our nerves fried before we get out of the mines..." Zachtia muttered.

"No touching the stones!" said Endia. "Each Mica is a death trap!"

"Very good." Dalian threw the stone over his shoulder, causing the stone it crashed into to flip over, and a jet of flame spewed forth and scorched the cavern's ceiling before dying to the floor from whence it came.

Dalian's expression never changed, but his voice cracked as he said, "Case in point. Let's move."

They continued on, careful of where they tread. Even Aldrin concentrated so much that he uttered few words.

Dalian was another story. "How many here would like to know the history of the Goblyns?"

"I do!" said Endia, immediately afterward looking back at her feet.

"I'm interested," said Aldrin.

"I'm outvoted," moaned Zachtia.

Dalian seemed to enjoy the last remark and began:

"During the Second Age in the reign of Dalaclamese II --"

Endia interrupted, "Wait, there was a king ruling at this time?"

"Emperor, actually," said Dalian. "He was a Blue elf, too. This is before the Great Enmity, the end of which the tribes decided to make a Council to govern the lands. Anyway…" Dalian looked up at the tunnel ceiling. "We of the Black Elf tribe found inscriptions that detail this history. They were in the language that you read,

Aldrin. With the help of Hunter, we were able to translate all the language. Some of us know how to speak it.

"Underground, under the empire of Dalaclamese, there was an Empire of Stone: the Goblyn empire. The Goblyns were a strange race, but a thriving one nonetheless: the history tells of miles upon miles of housing carved directly into the walls or etched from the ground, this being their main city complex. Families lived here, jobs were carried out here...a living was made." Dalian paused. "Heh...an entire civilization underneath the high and mighty elves."

Here, he stopped. "In fact, we should be entering the first section of the city in a moment. Mind your feet."

The tunnel suddenly became wider and Aldrin could make out two pillars on either side of them about a foot from each wall. Both of them had a divot in the middle.

"Aldrin," Dalian instructed, "I need another Lumen."

Aldrin fished out another Lumen from the backpack and handed it to Dalian, who in turn struck it on the left wall, illuminating the tunnel more than ever. He scraped the other one and refreshed the light. "I never get tired of this," he said eagerly under his breath. "Watch."

He placed one Lumen in the divot of the left pillar, then the other...and a chain reaction happened. Now Aldrin could see there was a stream of blue crystal imbedded in the pillar via the designs on the pillar and connected with a blue trail about a foot across that went in front of them. In a few seconds, the light of the Lumen ebbed and flowed like a river through the trail of blue crystal, brightening up the tunnel.

...then it looked as if the light stopped.

"What's with the light?" asked Zachtia.

"Wait a moment and follow me," Dalian said evenly and proceeded forward, the three other elves in tow.

He got to where he was about a foot where the trail seemed to end and stopped. "Here we are."

All three stopped right behind him and witnessed what was happening: the trails had not stopped but instead had gone straight down the face of the drop-off they were standing on! They were still going as the three realized where they were and the "rivers of blue" were travelling quickly. In a few seconds however, both trails hit bottom and split into four more trails afterward, illuminating even more of the tunnel which by now had widened astronomically, becoming more of a cavern.

From the way the light was obstructed, Aldrin could make out that there was a large bridge about what the size of the tunnel was originally. As the light kept going, now in thirty-two streams, Aldrin could see that the cavern went about a mile, the bridge reaching the other side, being held up by humongous buttresses made of what appeared to be solid rock. Honed into the buttresses were stairwells that were about a person across, spiraling down to the bottom.

Down in the base of the cavern was the scene that Dalian described: houses honed out of solid rock, splayed out in lines hundreds of units across. On the walls were more elaborate housing units with stairwells connecting them to each other and to the ground below.

The rivers of light now traveled upward, the majority of the lines travelling all the way to the ceiling, making large spirals until they could spiral no further and stopped.

Two lines continued on through to the other side of the bridge, ending on duplicate pillars in a tunnel that looked similar to the one they were in now. In the middle, something huge was blocking their view of the exact center.

Endia was the first one to break the silence. "...that's what's with the lights..."

"Yes, but there's a two-day time limit," said Dalian. "If not, I'd give you a grand tour of the place -- fascinating. But we'll only be able to see about 1/4th of it."

Endia looked crestfallen and Zachtia said, "Wait, why are we going to be seeing it at all, other than here?"

Dalian pointed to the bridge. "We found out that this bridge was built precisely to keep nosy outsiders from going any further. The elves -- or whatever -- that saw their companions get flattened, spiked, and otherwise mutilated would go down the stairs until they got to the city, where they would be promptly arrested, led to the surface, and turned loose with their hands tied behind their back and an arrow lodged in their right leg."

"Disgusting and unneeded!" cried Zachtia. "So, we need to go through the city to avoid being made into an elven broth."

"Precisely," Dalian said with a wry smile, "and I'm sure that you can make those conclusions for yourself in the future, unless you want more unneeded facts."

Zachtia made a face at him and Endia said under her breath, "I want to have some more unneeded facts..."

Dalian started on the bridge. "Well, you will probably get some more," he said, sounding sympathetic. "It's about a day's journey through the city and there are a few more things we have to watch out for. Come on."

Aside

The jail lay in pieces.

It had never been a good jail, though its warden was a good man. Officials removed his body from the crumpled wreckage and most of the valuables, what there were of them, had been cleared away. Now, Captain Dairlo, on indefinite leave for bravery, crouched beside what once was the far wall, gazing intently at the coin resting in his hand. "And the Green did this?" he asked his new companion.

The young, blond-haired noble, whom Dairlo had immediately taken a disliking to, nodded curtly. "I had just bid him and his confederates goodbye and good riddance and was leaving with my entourage, when suddenly the entire building started to give way and collapse in on itself. I turn around and see him carrying your wife like a sack of potatoes to a tree, dump her on the ground, and then attack my fellows and me."

Dairlo was silent for the moment, replaying the scene per the noble's description, and comparing it to what he had observed. "I'm sorry, master 'Ihar," he said, standing up and facing the noble with deadly eyes. "But that doesn't ring true. What really happened?"

"You dare!" the noble blustered, reddening. "I can have you arrested for that; I pay for your war supplies, Captain."

"And where would you put me?" asked the Red captain with an insincere smile. "Your jail has been torn down. Aleborne was murdered. There are signs of a fire, with remains of a wagon that just happened to be trundled in there." He took a step forward, and the noble backed away. Dairlo's voice was low, like the thunder of an oncoming storm. "What really happened, master 'Ihar," he repeated, the "master" coming out like a slap in the face. "Where are they now? Where is my wife?"

The noble just stood there, staring at Dairlo as if the captain was a bear about to eat him. Then, in a whiny voice he exclaimed, "I don't know, Creator confound me, I don't know, Captain!" his face was as red as Dairlo's uniform as his voice became angry again, "I ran for the town to gather more men to execute all of them, especially that Green."

Dairlo was about to chide him for running away when his mind locked on a phrase. "All of them," he said quietly.

"Yeah, the short one too," 'Ihar sniffed, not paying attention to the whitening knuckles of the Captain's fists. "Little Yellow miss, I'dve like to-"

His jaw suddenly went sideways as his face followed a split second later, driven hard into by Dairlo's fist.

The husband of Zachtia was considering finishing the job and his career forever when a female voice rang clearly, "Peace, Captain Dairlo'Ecduv'Demallahush... though you have the right idea."

A Warrior's Code

The voice sounded as if it came from right next to him, but when he turned to his right, he found the woman coming towards him was still a few yards away. She was clothed in white, her garb covering her entire body, with a hood over her head and a sash covering her mouth.

She was walking quickly over to him and walked past him, standing over the noble, who by now was looking up at both of them indignantly. His mouth was bleeding and there were tears streaming down his face. "Get away, woman," he said, trying to scramble away on the rough ground and failing miserably. "You and the captain here are both in trouble; there'll be an inquiry!"

The woman simply reached down and picked him up by the neck with one hand. "That's enough, Bairn'Ihar," she said with the same kind of thunderous quiet Dairlo had had a moment before. "You will sleep now."

Her back was turned to Dairlo, but he was watching the noble's face as it contorted in a paroxysm of fear... and then the young man's head lolled sideways, eyes rolling back and closing.

The woman set the man on his backside and let him fall flat on his back.

Dairlo was curious. "What was that technique?" he asked.

"It's an old gardening technique," she said. "Weeding out the fools." It sounded to the captain like her voice was rasping more. She tilted slightly forward and breathed in quickly. "That's better," she said under her breath and righting herself. She then turned to him and dropped her hood, pulling the sash away a moment later.

Dairlo looked at the familiar face with bountiful curls of brown hair framing it. "Gardener," breathed, bowing to the ancient young woman. "It's an honor. But why do you come here, counselor?"

"The same reason you are, Captain," the Gardener replied.

"You got a note as well?" asked Dairlo, surprised.

"No, but the news has reached me nevertheless," replied the woman, smiling.

"Then please tell me," furthered Dairlo tiredly. "Where is my wife?"

"She is safe," replied the Council member after a while and then continued, "She is with friends, walking a clear path under the Wanderer's Bane. I was actually on the way to meet them myself. I know where I will meet them, or at least him." Her face hardened. "But your place is back in the city where your wife will be overjoyed to meet you. The Green, Aldrin of Emeretl is guarding her like she is his own wife. He does not think this, mind you, for his love is with another."

Dairlo nodded thoughtfully and then blanched in a horrible realization. "Creator save us - Emeretl is that town Admiral Farnabach sai-"

"Wait for your wife to tell you, she will have plenty to say," the woman said with a shake of her hand.

He gave her a look. "That doesn't sound like her," he said slowly.

"Let's just say that she has found a practical use for... thorough conversation," the elf in white said with a quick smile. "By the time you get back to Scarlesh, she'll almost be there. Take the Southeast Route through the Satin Trails." She pulled something

shiny, flat, and round out of nowhere - Dairlo guessed she must have palmed it when he hadn't been looking - and handed it to him. "Take this. You'll need it when the time comes. Go."

Chapter 12

Aldrin took in the sights with eyes wide and mouth agape. The houses seemed to have been carved out of one piece of stone. As they travelled, he took every opportunity to look at the many intricate designs etched about the outside walls. "These are gorgeous," he said softly, running his hand along one of the spirals. "Are these just artistic or do they serve a purpose?" he asked Dalian.

"Oh, they serve a purpose," Dalian explained, moving on, forcing Aldrin to follow. "This was a bit of symbol language, making up a sort of coat of arms. See here..." he pointed at the house he was passing to the left of him. "See how the spiral takes a turn to the left after about three circles? That signifies the male was the third child of his household -- a great honor. The line continues a few inches and does a two-circle spiral in the other direction. His wife was the second child of her family." Dalian smiled. "They had two children, judging by the small spirals connected with the mother's line."

Now everyone had stopped. They watched as Dalian felt the wall as if he was mesmerized by it. "What happened to them?" Endia asked softly.

The answer she got was not the one she expected. "They were gathering food when the fire started," Dalian said softly. "The fire scattered into the field. The two young ones ran to their mother and they all ran from the house. They were captured by a Purple group and were taken from the Bane. When I heard what had happened, I assembled a team, hunted the Purples down and wiped them from existence. But my family was gone."

He chuckled and the sound sent chills down their spines. "So, they might have made it. They might have been eaten. I don't know. It's a wonderful guessing game. I keep myself up thinking about it."

Aldrin cautiously walked over to Dalian and put his hand on the elf's shoulder.

The action made Dalian straighten up. "Right!" he said. "No time for nostalgia or insanity, eh? Besides, you...were asking about the Goblyns. Moving on..."

Zachtia and Aldrin exchanged glances and followed Dalian as the elf continued forth. "The Goblyns had a society of peace, barring their love of traps. Their economy was based on trade -- but they had something that was the key to their peace. It was a room where time seemed to reflect upon itself perfectly."

Aldrin squinted. "A prophecy room?"

"Exactly. They hung the biggest cutting of onyx they could find at the peak of the time reflection, and believe you me, when you see it...you'll realize why they called it the Time Mirror."

Dalian twirled around and walked backwards. "Now, being a clever race, the Goblyns decided to trap this room as well. They placed four mica cuttings around the stone and the reflection of time was just strong enough and just scattered enough that they had one true Mirror of Time...and four false Mirrors of Time. Each of the 'mirrors' gave a reflection of the future...but only one of them was the right one."

They walked in silence for a few hours after this and passed many more houses. Aldrin could deduce that there were some hospitals they passed, some gated communities -- there were stone walls around groupings of houses with gates in them -- and other "modern" housings.

They passed what appeared to be a steeple from the City of the Council. "Who did the Goblyns worship?" he asked Dalian softly. The more open and empty the space, the more one wanted to whisper. "I know most of us worship the Creator…what about these people?"

Dalian looked at the steeple himself. "As far as we can tell, there were some sects. Some worshiped the creator in some form or fashion, but most worshiped Magnos, their god of bountiful creation and earth, also Laph, goddess of cleverness…"

They went on like this for hours, to Zachtia's dismay. They talked about the Goblyn's culture, economy, and the other gods of their society. To be honest, she did not find it as annoying as she did when she first started this journey. Indeed, she had seen that the only logical course of action was to enjoy it - or simply let it happen. Still, she could not ignore her Red predilection for silence. Like it or not, "mounds of talking". as Aldrin had put it, made her uncomfortable.

She now concluded that the elf leading them on this half-tour, half-shortcut could not have been a Red elf in his past life. He talked too much, simple as that! Any self-respecting Red would be averse to the notion. Even battle plans could be fit on one page.

She found the Goblyn city a trifle disturbing. Images dredged up from childhood stories kept flittering around in her mind; stories of ghosts…spirits of the unsettled dead. It did not take much imagination to begin to see shadows in her peripheral vision, disappearing into doorways or around corners. She would be quite glad when they were out.

A Warrior's Code

In the clearing ahead, they could now make out what was previously in darkness, the very large cylinder they had observed when they started making their way down. It was a very tall building, more like one of the buttresses that supported the high ceiling above. Of course, Aldrin knew that if it was hollowed out as a building, it was more of an extravagant decor than anything. The building part itself looked like a stylized tree, large enough that spiral staircases could be used on the outside of the building. The branches of the "tree" curled up into the ceiling, while the "roots" struck out on all sides, dozens of them, some open on top, others sealed off, but almost every single one of them were interconnected with each other. Up near the center of the building, Aldrin could see there were much smaller windows, but unlike all the other windows, which were dark and quite baleful, they were glowing with an eerie light that seemed to flicker, like a candle.

Dalian asked for another Lumen, making the Green snap out of his reverence. Aldrin was a little slower in fishing out this. "Seems to be the last one," he finally said, handing the stone to their guide.

"It'll be enough," said their guide, dropping the spent Lumen he had been using like a torch - which was still glowing but weakly - and scraping the new luminescent rock against the wall they had been following. "When we get to the exact center of the city, there will be no need for artificial illumination on our part."

Their trek had led them to where the "roots" ended as paths with two walls alongside them, blocking them off from the rest of the Mines. They entered a rather large one. Aldrin had not judged the vastness of the two sides of the roots correctly at first, but he now saw they were as tall as the trees in the Trepidation Forest. He had a hard time not stopping and taking in the sight.

A Warrior's Code

Dalian was still playing the tour guide. Aldrin really thought the elf was a Green. So much energy under control - whether by depression or by actual mental control - and the information he was giving sounded as if he was actually excited to be giving the info. "The gardens, as best as we can figure out," he informed them. "Soil samples were very rich here when we explored. You can also see that there is an abnormal amount of subterranean flora starting here." His speech sounded a little distracted. "Also..." His face brightened a little as he raised the Lumen over where the soil started.

The three other elves all gave utterances of astonishment as the soil itself began to shine and sparkle. "Are diamonds mixed in with the soil?"" asked Endia, making a guess.

"It's too bright for that," muttered Aldrin. He bent down and withdrew a handful of the soil, letting it sift through his hands, studying it. "I would venture to guess it's more of a type of Lumen, ground into dust." He concentrated at his right side, feeling around with his hand. "I know it's here somewhere," he said softly to himself, feeling around in his displaced bag of miscellaneous objects.

"Aldrin," said Dalian, "I know this is interesting..." He watched as Aldrin finally pulled out an empty, corked bottle and began filling it with the bioluminescent sand. "But have you forgotten your pursuer?"

Aldrin started, straightening. "The Purple," he said. In the excitement and wonder of the moment, the Purple had slipped from the forefront of his mind.

Dalian nodded. "He's close enough I can faintly sense him. With any luck, he'll trip on one of the Mica stones and die in the mines. But I'm not going to be here when you face him."

"Coward!"" barked Zachtia.

"'Realist' I believe is the word you're looking for," said Dalian, unmoved. "This Purple is your battle - your problem, not mine, and besides, Hunter said he wouldn't fight your battles, let alone have me fight them."

Aldrin had re-corked his bottle, his expression more serious than ever. "You're right, we need to keep moving," he said. "Especially since it seems the only way to get to the other side is going through that tower."

"Mythology again?" asked Dalian, eyebrow up.

"Observation," replied the Green elf.

"In any case, you're right. There is an alternate route through the 'suburbs', of the mines, but that would take too long. Besides, there is something I have been asked to show you in the tower."

"The so-called "Prophecy Room"?" Aldrin guessed.

"Precisely."

They continued forward. As they did so, some roots seemed to coalesce with each other, then branch off separate ways. Mysteriously, this place seemed much brighter than any of the other places they had visited even if it didn't have the glowing soil, and overhead there were what looked like stars. "The 'garden spot' was a maze of sorts, fairly easy, since all the roads lead to the tower," Dalian explained. "As far as we can tell, since it couldn't be a tourist attraction, it was a tranquil, cerebral place."

Endia once again could be mistaken for a small child as she looked around but stayed close to Aldrin. "For a garden spot, this is

huge!" she said softly. "Kind of like what Dema'Kay described in his
Terabinthian Heights and other Ancient Grounds."

"Yeah it's huge," Zachtia muttered, stabilizing herself. Her
child was not handling this intrusion to its peace too kindly and the
few rests that she had been given were barely sufficient. She looked
up at the towering walls, that almost encased them. "If I were
planning a garden, I'd probably would have had it open. How did
they suppose they'd grow anything here?"

In response, Dalian snatched up a piece of rubble in the road,
and - still walking - flung it high. It struck what had looked like one
of the stars, and immediately there was a shattering sound. Both
female elves jumped as what looked like impossibly thin metal as
shiny as water came scattering down. "That reflected the
illuminescence of the cave," the Black elf called back. "It's also why
this narrow way is as bright as it is."

They did not object, though Zachtia scowled at him. "Why
do we need to go to this tower, anyway?"

"Didn't I already tell you?" asked Dalian, surprised. "The
suburbs would take too long."

"Yes, but why this 'Prophecy Room'?" pushed Zachtia, "Why
do we need to see that?"

This time it was Aldrin who spoke up, addressing Dalian,
"Do we know if the Prophecy Room showed the future of a specific
location?"

"You're a Green," started Dalian, but before he could
continue with "you figure it out", Aldrin interrupted softly, "So are
you."

Dalian stopped walking and slowly turned to Aldrin. His face was calm. "I'm of the Black Tribe," he said.

"But you *were* a Green, Dalian," said Aldrin, taking a step closer. "Is this fact shameful to you?"

Dalian said nothing, just stared at Aldrin.

Aldrin continued. "You were in the Daquarus Section of the Bacht, exploration with the Yellows. You lost communication with us after you entered the Goblyn Mines." He tilted his head. "Or was communication severed?"

"Aldrin, stop," Zachtia cautioned softly.

Aldrin seemed to ignore her. "You dealt with your family being gone in the only way you could." His voice had sunk. "You went into seclusion. You found such a mental connection with the Black Tribe that you couldn't tear yourself away. Tell me…what happened to the Yellow elves?"

His eyes were searching the cold eyes of the so-said Black elf. Finally, Dalian sighed. "…we needed their information. They were absorbed, one after another, every two weeks."

"You had a code of honor!" roared Aldrin, his suddenly loud voice echoing throughout the deserted Mines. "You vowed to protect your charge, not *sacrifice* them for nourishment or knowledge!"

The voice of the other elf was half as loud but just as serious, "I had severed my ties with the Green Tribe, my honor and my conscience lie with the Black Elves. Besides - " Dalian suddenly interrupted himself, " - and how could you have not noticed what was intrinsically obvious about that place, Aldrin? That undercurrent?"

Aldrin breathed out a deep breath. He felt Zachtia at his arm, holding it gently. Endia was still astonished at what had been revealed that for once she had remained silent. Aldrin finally replied in a croaking voice, "…that feeling of home? Yes. I remember. I felt it. I'm sure everyone else felt it. But the difference between you and us, Dalian, is that Endia has her father, Zachtia has her husband, and I…" For a moment he had to steady himself. "…I have a duty to both. They have become my family. You - you had it in your mind you had no one left. Even if you had a lingering hope that your family was still alive, the rest of you was in deep depression. So when that feeling of coming home and the warmth of it all hit you like a tidal wave, you succumbed to it. Feeding from Hunter's ability just strengthened that bond - pulled you deeper into it." He gave a deep, ragged sigh. "You interrupted yourself. You said besides. What 'besides' was there?"

"They always died willingly."

Endia finally found her speech. "The Daquarus division of the Yellow Tribe consisted of all uncoupled elves. When they hit that 'homely' mental carrier-wave…"

"They did the same thing that Dalian here did," Aldrin finished. "They shed their colors and succumbed to the Black Tribe's 'family'."

Everyone was silent for a few moments. Zachtia was still holding Aldrin's arm. Endia had remained where she stood, still pondering the mound of information before them. Finally, it was Aldrin that broke the silence. "Then, I am still the last of the Green elves," he sighed softly. "A pity." He set his jaw and looked at Dalian. "We're wasting precious time - lead on."

A Warrior's Code

Dalian nodded and turned…but then looked over his shoulder. "…the family you now have Aldrin," he said softly, "…I think it's just as good as mine."

Chapter 13

After the incident with Dalian and the revealing of his identity, the group was quite quiet. There was no tension, though - indeed, the outburst of information had put everyone a little more at ease; Aldrin with his knowledge of Dalian, Zachtia with her doubts about him, and Endia with her wonder of the entire situation.

They finally got to the base of the structure, though they could only tell because the "root" they had been following closed on ahead into a doorway. Eerie light showed through the doorway - though the entire structure now had an eeriness about it. Decay was almost nonexistent here.

And yet it was existent.

Aldrin studied the archway of the door closely, watching the structure. It shifted ever so slightly, but not in space. It was as if it was shuddering into decay, and then shuddering back anew. He reached out a hand and placed it firmly against the rock and was amazed at the sensations. It felt as if the rock were solid water - like ice but not as cold, and it moved and tingled as it grew older and yet simultaneously younger. "Incredible," he breathed.

Endia had followed Aldrin's actions and was almost up against him. "...I've never seen anything like this," she said softly. She was nervous. That glow in the doorway warned her that something was still living here. But the Mines had been empty for...centuries? Millennia? Even she did not know.

Zachtia was resting against the wall, her entire back against the shifting rocks. "This feels really, *really* strange," she said, frowning. She looked at Dalian, who had parted a little from the group to observe them and looked like he was enjoying their explorations. "Do you know why it's doing that?"

Before Dalian could answer, Aldrin stood up and said, "I'm going to call it magic."

Endia looked up at him, eyes wide. "But magic is evil, remember? You said that the Blues were turned to Purples because of magic."

"That magic, yes…" He pondered for a moment. "But just think about it. Our ancestors believed in magic, yes? We found that most of what they thought was magic was actually nature working how it was supposed to work. Displacement, we almost called it magic. But our scientists believe it to be that if you pass through the microstructures of our reality, you enter a sub-reality. There might even be a time when an elf could displace himself - I read about experiments they did back in the Four Towers Library."

"Exciting, Aldrin," said Zachtia a little urgently, "But could you get back to the explanation before our pursuer gets here? Why do you call it magic?"

"I call it magic because, for right now, there is no scientific explanation," said Aldrin. "It's something that the Creator made that doesn't follow our logic, so therefore it's 'magic.'"

Dalian, who had been listening all the while, nodded. "That's a very fair explanation, Aldrin - logical, succinct, but I believe I can trump you with a little bit of Black Elf explanation." He walked over to the group, who immediately gave their attention. "This place," he explained, "Is right next to a time-rift. It's called the *Telvennan Anachronistic Effect,* though only seen happening here."

No one responded for a while. Finally, Aldrin's eyes brightened, and he said, "Telvenna's *Anachronisms*."

"Of course!" cried Endia, jumping up and down in childish excitement. "I see now - I read it, but I didn't really think it was possible!"

Once again, Zachtia interrupted, "So it sounds like I need to catch up on my reading - could someone please fill me in on this big realization?!"

"Think of time as a fast-running river," Aldrin said, moving his fingers in a horizontal fashion to illustrate. "It only moves one direction, and all the fish have to go a certain way. The Green elf and Yellow elf Telvenna - both had the same name, you see, so they worked as a team - postulated that just as a large body of water - as time has to be, though still a river - has eddies and undercurrents that move different directions, time would also have eddies and undercurrents - places where time seemed to pass more quickly or more slowly. They also postulated that the river of time could be diverted, and *that* is what the rift is. Time is being diverted back on itself, flowing in the same direction but water from downstream is finding itself flowing upstream, looping back and flowing again."

"Only partially," added Dalian. "Time is still flowing on regardless of interruption. It's like we are experiencing an echo of what happened, but we can feel it and touch it. Like a windup toy going through its movements with all its gears, always making the same movement. You can nudge it as well as you like, but it will always go through that same movement."

Zachtia took in this information as best as she could, though honestly most of it went over her head. Endia, on the other hand, always had that look of comprehension and excitement. "We're experiencing the *Anachronistic Happenstance* that the two Telvenna's talked about."

"Except it's a little different," said Dalian, sounding just the slightest unnerved. "Their postulations sounded like it was all smooth and graceful. As we get up into the tower, you'll see that it's almost - what's the word for it -*unbalanced*...though I figure that it's the Mica."

Aldrin blinked. "The stones? I thought they just reflected time..." His eyes now widened as he nodded owlishly. "I see."

Zachtia gave him a glower. "Again, left out," she said in an undeniably irritated voice. "Still a Red here!"

This time it was Endia that piped up. "The Mica and Onyx stones are not only showing pictorial reflections of time, but they're what is keeping the rift looping after all these years! The Onyx probably isn't doing any harm, it's the Mica that is making everything all..." she looked at Dalian. "'Unbalanced,' as you said? So...it's like there are rocks in the stream?"

"Very loosely like, yes," shrugged Dalian, sounding helpless for another explanation. "Some parts of time are just shadows, like ghosts. Others I could have sworn looked at me as I traveled up, and others were tangible only for a time until the loop reset."

"*Looked at you?*" Aldrin quoted. "Then there are...we're going to -"

"Be seeing the Goblyns face-to-face, though they won't be able to see us, most of them," Dalian said. "They are shadows of the past, looping in from different times. There are obstacles that we have to face before we get to the actual Prophecy Room, so be wary."

"Now you tell us," muttered Zachtia, though it was not that that had captured her interest.

Aldrin looked at her. "Something wrong?"

"No...maybe," she said. "I thought I saw ghosts while we traveled. I didn't say anything because I thought it was just my imagination playing tricks on me in this disturbing place. ...maybe not."

Dalian nodded slowly, looking at the two of them. "You could very well have seen a glimmer of the past," he said softly. He cleared his throat. "Come on," he said a little louder, "Let's get to it."

The whole place had a closed-in silence about it. Not the open space, atmospheric aura of silence that the cavern had, but a boxed in, eerie silence. Except for the pattering of the feet of the elves and their breathing, and their heartbeats, there was no other sound of any kind, and all sounds seemed to echo about the building.

They had entered the "tree" and were looking up at what was before them. The walls were several feet thick, so the structure acted as a buttress and not just as décor as Aldrin had surmised. However, when they had gotten past the thick entranceway, they were greeted by what was to them a gigantic hall. Circular and enchanting, the designs and structure of this one floor would be an architect's dream come true. Claiming the gaze of the travelers were the columns that kept the ceiling up about thirty feet above their heads. What made them the center of attention were the intricate designs and carvings in them: carvings of Goblyns.

Here was the ancient race carved in stone. Their sharp, oval faces had sunken, big, slitted eyes, very proud and graceful. Their noses were raised ridges with holes at the end, under which were small mouths, some of which were open to reveal rows of sharp teeth. Their ears were larger than elves' ears, still pointed, but a little rounder and more towards the top of the head than on either side.

Most of the carvings were female, their forms either in a dancing pose or else a warrior's pose. The clothing complimented each pose, either armor and what appeared to be leather skirts and hoods, or else capes flowing about them and other alluring trappings.

The male carvings were mostly of warriors, some of them even having bows and arrows jutting out of the column they had been rendered into. Others looked to be like servants in loincloths, carrying bowls or fruit.

"A masterfully artistic people," said Dalian, barely above a whisper. "As if you already couldn't tell."

Aldrin was admiring the craftsmanship and pose of what appeared to be a younger Goblyn male, down on one knee, offering up a goblet to an unseen master. "They all appear to be quite fit," he observed, "though it could be just the artist's preference."

"Come along," said Dalian with the force of a tutor with a daydreaming student. "You'll have plenty of Goblyns to observe once we get upstairs, they rarely visited down here…hah!" He suddenly pointed excitedly to the left of Aldrin, and they all turned.

There, standing before them, was a very young Goblyn female. They could see now that the Goblyn's skin was brownish and scruffy, like leather. She held a slate of smooth rock in her hand and on it was a sheet of paper. She seemed to be staring straight at Aldrin with deep blue eyes, but when Aldrin moved experimentally, her eyes never followed. "She's looking at the statue," he said almost inaudibly. He walked over to her and went behind her, looking at the sheet of paper. He observed the tool in her hand as she drew on the paper, the object a thin cylinder of apparently black rock, but when she moved it across the paper, it left a mark.

"Intriguing," he said. He gave the image on the paper and the statue a quick comparison and then looked at his wide-eyed companions. "Not bad," he said with a smile.

…and then gave a gasp as the girl disappeared. He looked at the spot where she had been, cautiously moved a hand around where her head had been, and then finally looked at Dalian. "The *Happenstance*," he whispered.

Dalian nodded with a small smile. "She'll reappear in a few moments, her drawing reset. She'll make those continuing strokes and then disappear, resetting once again a few moments later."

Zachtia shuddered. "I'm glad she knows nothing about it - does she?"

"She can't, considering she's a happening of the past," deduced Endia. "To her, she's already finished the picture, grown up, gotten married, had children, I dunno. We're just looping on one moment of her life."

Dalian nodded, smiling. "A fine string of thought, Miss Yellow, though I wouldn't expect less," he said. "But, we are wasting time." He pointed as he walked to a staircase that hugged the wall, made from wood. "This is our only way up."

Endia overtook him and felt up the railing. "It's wood alright!" she said, fascinated. "Though how it's stayed like this I haven't the faintest. It should have disintegrated with age." She suddenly gave a yelp as the structure changed under her searching hands. It cracked and ebbed, the glossy finish now shuddering into a dismally rough and splintering mess. The wood groaned inaudibly under the ages as its infrastructure faltered, and finally...the staircase vanished altogether.

Endia took a step backward, glancing between her companions and where the structure had been. "...Um, so that happened," she said in a confused voice.

All nodded except for Dalian, who had closed his eyes and tilted his head back, muttering under his breath.

"Okay, so how are we going to get up there now?" asked Zachtia in an exasperated voice.

Aldrin held up a hand and stared at Dalian. "You said the girl would reappear," he said.

"34, 33 - that's right - 32, 31," confirmed Dalian.

"So therefore, if the girl will reappear," continued Aldrin, "it stands to reason that the staircase will as well."

"25, you got it...23."

Zachtia huffed, "What's with the counting?"

Aldrin gave her a glance. "Isn't it obvious? He's counting down until the staircase reappears."

"15, quite correct, 13," said Dalian.

They all waited and listened until he said, "five, four three, two, one," and clicked his tongue.

Seemingly at the sound, the staircase, now shinier and newer than it was before, came back into existence, as if it had never left.

Dalian swept his hand up. "Shall we continue?"

A Warrior's Code

They quickly ran up the stairs, Zachtia having a harder time with the life in her womb being extra weight for the usually light elves. Dalian was the first one up on the second floor, motioning them to keep coming. Endia could not help but notice the stairway slowly getting older as they climbed up it. She quickened her pace until she ran up beside Aldrin and almost passed him. They all made it up and looked at Dalian with expectation.

One could not help but see the stress now pictured in his face. Aldrin was the first to speak up. "What's wrong?"

"That was easy..." Dalian began.

"Speak for yourself," panted Zachtia, giving him a glare. "You don't have a boulder-sack of a stomach."

"Not what I mean," continued Dalian. "That was easy - compared to what's up ahead."

Zachtia groaned, and Endia asked in her excited fashion, "How so?"

"That staircase lasts for about five minutes," explained Dalian softly. "Might get a little rickety towards the fifth but it holds strong until that time, then it disappears. There are more like it - not just staircases but doorways that move, floors that crumble, and there are even some Goblyns we have to dodge - and we'll have to move fast. I cannot emphasize this *enough*. Each floor has an element of danger in it, if we're on a staircase or a floor and it disappears, we'll drop. If a doorway disappears in the middle of our walking through it - I don't know, but I shudder to think of what happens when solid matter meets solid matter."

Zachtia's eyes were wide. "How many floors are we talking here?"

Dalian craned his neck, eyes rolled up in thought. He finally looked back down with a grimace. "47," he said in a hesitating voice.

Zachtia looked at him with a contemplative expression. "…I need to sit down," she groaned as she almost fell onto the stone floor.

Dalian then went on to go into detail about the obstacles that they would encounter. Aldrin made a mental list of everything, including the times. Dalian had explained that he had timed each happenstance and the time it took for them to appear, disappear, and reappear. Zachtia listened with a mild shock and tried to keep track of each occurrence, but failed miserably. In truth, she was praying that the Creator would keep her going and not pass out like she thought more likely. Endia was keeping a list too, though it was a little harder for her. Her apprehension had grown a little as she listened to some of the very short times they had before the object they were crossing collapsed or disappeared.

"The 35th floor will be the hardest," Dalian was saying. "Not because of it's shortness in time, but because of its increased time and insufficient room."

"How insufficient?" came Zachtia's tired voice from the floor.

"A group of four elves have to stand where two would be comfortable," Dalian explained. "We will have time to regroup and observe it on the floor below, but it's being there and not dropping thirty-plus feet for forty-five seconds that's going to be hard."

"But at least we'll be stationary," said Zachtia with some hope.

"Yes, and have the same breathing space as a pile of fish caught in a net," added Dalian to Zachtia's dismay.

Dalian nodded as Aldrin looked around at this floor. This was another grand floor, having no walls to contend with, only the stairs on the other side. It looked like it was a reception area, with tables laid out in the center of the room like on the bottom floor of the Four Towers library. "Is this where they checked in?" he asked, at a loss for words.

Dalian gave him a look. "They lived here," he said. "At least all the military did."

"The military lived here?" asked Zachtia. "The military lived in the Prophecy Towers?"

"The military, their immediate families, and the king himself," explained Dalian. Aldrin noticed that Dalian wasn't looking around the room, but his eyes were cast on the floor itself, which consisted of slabs of stone. He also heard a faint creaking and scraping, like stone and wood were being ground together far away.

Dalian continued, "From what we can tell, the King housed his armies at these bottom floors, the higher ranks getting higher into the tower until you got to just below the Prophecy Room where he and his family lived. At Level 26 there's a colossal dining room, and at level 27 – ah, there they go."

Aldrin's eyes had been on Dalian but now snapped to the floor again. The stone slabs had been getting louder with the sound and suddenly, without warning, began to drop in groups to the floor below! The benches and tables that had been creaking and groaning all this time came apart and fell into the maw the falling stones had made.

Aldrin and Endia immediately jerked back until they were flat against the wall, noticing only then that Dalian was staring at them with an eyebrow raised. "It's perfectly safe," he said. "If you stay near the stairs."

Zachtia glared at him, having tried to scoot up against the wall and succeeded in getting the backside of her dress all musty. "You could have warned us. Again!" she snarled grumpily.

"Fine, fine," Dalian relented, shrugging. "I'll warn you all when something's about to happen from now on. It's just so fun seeing your reactions."

Aldrin heard Zachtia mutter something about "sadist" under her breath, but he ignored it.

They watched as only the stones that were held up by the buttress statues stayed intact. Aldrin noticed with his Green fascination that, though they had plunged to the floor below, they had disappeared before reaching the bottom. Was it part of the "rules" of the *Happenstance*? As in each level was in its own time-zone? He pondered this until the slabs reappeared and Dalian started walking towards the stairs, motioning towards the group. "Let's keep moving," he said. "We still have 45 levels to go."

(To keep his report brief, Aldrin mentioned only thirteen floors that were more interesting than the rest. He passed up the floors that only had steps blinking in and out of existence, one or two stones in the floor giving way, and he passed up most of the floors of the barracks. This chronology will follow suit.)

Level 10

It was Endia who first picked up the sound as they made their way through a solid-stone stair shaft. "I hear voices," she whispered to Dalian in front of her, who in turn nodded.

"This is the first of the more interesting floors," the Black Elf said in a hushed voice, "There's no time limit for this one."

"Ah, the 'whispers' floor?" asked Aldrin, his voice also hushed.

"Exactly," returned Dalian, looking back up the stairs as they were about to level out onto the floor.

Zachtia, who was in the middle of the group – Aldrin in the back and Endia in the front – piped up in a hissed whisper, "Care to elaborate?"

"The walls have been made with Mica stones embedded elaborately throughout them for decoration," explained Dalian, pausing just at the top at the stairs and looking back, "But they have had designs cut out from them and replaced with silver. As far as we can tell, that's what is keeping us from seeing the people who are making the noises, but we are hearing the voices of four distinct timelines. The first one is what sounds to be a school outing, going back down to the schooling floor we passed through earlier. The next is from the war when the Blue Elves invaded the Goblyn mines, and the next one is the occupation of the Elves before they left." He grimaced. "And echoes from my past. We don't want to add our voices to the mix, do we?" When given a unanimous shake of the head, he continued, "Right, so on this level we need to keep silent and listen." He looked at Aldrin with a wry expression. "It'll probably be the toughest floor for you."

Aldrin frowned at the elf, and together they all walked up from the stairs and into the large hallway.

It was if it was a wall of sound had hit them as soon as they stepped foot into the five-elf-wide, ten-foot tall hallway. Voices of an unknown language were laughing and talking all around them, and Aldrin found himself looking around for the many bodies of youngling Goblyns there must be all around him. They all sounded innocent, though on one occasion there sounded to be a scuffle, and Dalian signed to Aldrin something about "books" and "grumpy turn-around" – or that was what Aldrin got by the Bacht sign language.

It was both wonderful and unnerving to hear this commotion. The group did add a few sounds to this part of the area, for Endia – who was a child's height – gasped when a voice right near her ear burst into laughter.

When they made it about halfway through the hallway, the sounds abruptly changed. Aldrin had to bite his tongue to hold in a gasp as the sounds of swords clashing against each other and cries of fury and death raged about him. He looked at Dalian who signed the word "War." Zachtia gripped Aldrin's arm as they passed through this chaos.

Aldrin had a hard time not imagining the battle that had gone on millennia ago, Blue Elf against Goblyn, master warrior against master trickster. The memories of the war that had left him homeless wafted back into his mind and he in turn gripped Zachtia's hand. *Hang on,* he told himself. *This is not the place to have an episode. You're with family. This happened millennia ago. You are safe… for now.* Still, he stared at the back of Dalian's head fervently as they walked together, Endia at his side now, her arms gripping him about the waist. His mind was like a startled deer tied to a frayed rope, his breath quickening, and heart racing. His skin felt clammy and slippery as he fought to keep control.

Zachtia gave a shriek as an unseen spear flew just past Aldrin's nose, and they heard the cry of death as it found its target. Aldrin's eyes played with shadows and he went dizzy, seeing for an instant the image of a Goblyn slumped against the wall with a spear through his chest, eyes staring blankly at the elf, like so many of his friends of the war. He shook his head frantically, fighting the urge to run, to give into this irrational panic that was threatening to overtake him.

However, as they came within thirteen feet of the next staircase, the room became silent, much to Aldrin's relief. Then, as the group listened and neared the steps, they heard talking. Low voices came from the steps. Aldrin caught a glimpse of Dalian signing "Generals" and to calm his overly frazzled nerves he tried to listen in on the conversation as they passed the two talkers. Of course, it was in the Blue Elf's native language, but Aldrin discerned the words "quick," "King," and the interesting word "guardian."

When they got to the stairs and started to climb, the two murmuring voices ceased, to be replaced by,

"Yes, it's beautiful."

Aldrin's eyes darted to Dalian, who shook his head. It had been his voice alright, but he hadn't spoken.

Another voice followed soon after a deeper and more urgent voice, "I think we should go back, Dalian, we've explored too much as it is. I don't know how much time we have left on those Lumens."

"Oh, it's only been four hours," came Dalian's voice offhandedly. "And besides, Commander Antilien gave us six hours to return. Plenty of time to explore a little more and perhaps use the bridge on the other side as a shortcut."

"The group is probably waiting for us," insisted the other voice urgently. "Six hours was the longest time – they'll send up a search party next, and we barely survived the floor collapsing on the second floor!"

There was silence for a moment, and Dalian in the present waved to the group to hurry on. His voice said "Fine, have it your way," as they reached the middle of the stairs, and silence followed, leaving them once again alone in the tower.

Dalian turned to them. "We can rest now, it's safe here." He looked at Aldrin. "I did tell you that this would be the hardest on you," he said softly, his expression pained and sympathetic.

The Green elf nodded numbly, in an instant aware of tears streaming down his face.

Zachtia noticed this too, and she gasped. "Are you okay?" she asked urgently.

"Yes, um…" he stuttered. With a few more breaths to steady himself, he said quietly, "I will be." He shot a look at Dalian. "I thought you meant that I would find it hard not being able to comment on things."

Dalian grunted. "Well, there was that too. Come on, thirty-two floors to go." He turned but caught the glare of the two women elves, and he slumped, sighing. "Whenever you're ready."

Level 14

Endia gulped ruefully as they stared down the deep chasm that was before them. This spiral staircase, Dalian claimed, was a beneficial shortcut, compared to the executional aquarium they would have had to pass through to get to the other side. Now that she saw the obstacle, she somewhat wished they had decided to chance the ten seconds of purnara-fish packs.

The staircase they were on was in all rights a spiral staircase. The big difference was that it spiraled around the room that Dalian said the aquarium was in, meaning that it was two-elves wide with the room wall and the wall outside on both sides and the ceiling was over thirty feet above them. Nearing the end of the staircase, Dalian had stopped them short of a ten-foot gap in the middle of the stairway. Endia could now see that the metal stairs weren't being held up by anything, but the wall had been built so that the weight of the building was directly on it, therefore supporting it. However, a section of the thick wall tiles had apparently come loose, and the stairs that were being supported by them were gone.

"I'm guessing they won't reappear?" she moaned up to Dalian and he shook his head.

"These stairs had either fallen out of place or had been taken out of place before," he explained, the Yellow elf groaning again in response. "So, therefore, they decided, instead of replacing it, to put in something that would 'test the agility of the soldier.'" He pointed upwards about ten feet above the hole, and for a few moments, they saw nothing. Then a wooden bar with what looked like a noose dangling from it came into existence. "That's our way across," Dalian confirmed. "A good jump and full swing of both legs will get an adult elf all the way across."

Endia stared at the rope. "I can't jump that high," she said with a twinge of fear in her voice. "I'd fall."

"Yes, that's why I'm going to have Aldrin go first," Dalian said in a tone of voice that hinted she should have already figured this out, "and catch you when I heave you over like a boulder-shot."

"And what about my child and me?" asked Zachtia, faintly rubbing her bulging belly.

"Yes…" The Black elf thumbed his belt with a grimace. "We'll cross that bridge when we come to it."

"What does that even mean?" cried the Red elf tiredly. "We're already at the bridge, and the bridge isn't there! A noose is!" She shot the rope an angry look as if it had retorted. "I can barely run let alone jump in this disposition." She looked at Dalian with a petulant frown. "I'm stuck over here if the rope is our only option."

"I'm open to suggestions if you can think of any," Dalian said, his voice having a cold edge to it. "You keep saying you're a Red. Act like it."

Zachtia stood a little straighter, the grumpy expression now replaced by equal parts startled and furious expression. "Excuse me?" she said in a barely kept tone.

"Reds are the tactical geniuses," explained Dalian, his voice still in that cold humor. "If you hadn't spent the last several weeks walking around with someone who thinks of everything three months in advance, you probably would have already thought of a way to get over this obstacle."

"It's not that easy, and you know it!" snapped Zachtia angrily. "This isn't a battle map! There are no tactics to be planned out, no enemy! And by the way, I *sat in* on strategic discussions, my *husband* is the tactical genius." She gesticulated furiously at the gap, the rope having disappeared for the moment. "There's nothing I can plan out."

"Sure there is," said Dalian, his lax tone creeping back into his voice. "Your enemy is the gap. Your army is everything around you. Your battlefield is the rope. That's the difference between Green and Red thinking," he tapped his temple, "it's the lateral thinking."

She started to object, and then Dalian let her have it. "You said your husband was a tactical genius, but your husband isn't *here* right now. You'll just have to do."

Zachtia looked at him defiantly… and then turned away towards the gap.

Endia was in shock and Aldrin voiced her thoughts with quiet fury. "That. Was. *Low*. How could you have stooped so low and said that? You could have probably deduced with your ingenious little mind that she misses her husband deeply."

Then, before Dalian could retort, Zachtia's voice came in a hoarse whisper. "Belts."

She turned to Aldrin, eyes deadly serious and wet. She spoke again, her tone that of cold steel and resolve. "Your bow, one of your Buffalo arrows, and both of your belts." She turned the look on Dalian. "Now."

It didn't even take a minute for the two elves to scramble off their leather belts. Aldrin had a hard time getting his bow and the thick arrow together from their displaced spots – he was shocked at the tone of voice and deadly gleam in her eye that he hadn't seen during the entire trip.

She took the items and then looked at Endia. "I need one of your shoestrings, Endia," she said to the girl, her voice softer but nonetheless determined.

Endia dropped to one knee and fished one shoestring out of her shoe. By now the noose and wooden bar had disappeared until the next iteration, which would not take long to transpire.

Zachtia set down the bow and Dalian's belt and focused on the arrow, shoestring, and Aldrin's belt. She tied the belt buckle to the thick rod of the arrow with the shoestring and laced it around the sharp triangle tip of the arrow so the string and belt wouldn't come off. She then put Dalian's belt buckle on the end of Aldrin's and secured it onto the second hole to the end.

Then, gathering up the bow, she strung the arrow, pulled back, and waited.

Five seconds later, the noose returned. It was dangling about three inches higher than the Red elf's head and was suspended in the middle of the gap. She let loose the arrow, wincing as one of the flying belts caught her on the cheek.

The arrow flew through the eye of the noose, coming out the other side and dangling. While the other three elves watched in silence, she maneuvered the stringed belts so that she caught the arrow in her hand. She fumbled with the buckle of Aldrin's belt until she got it hooked into the first hole of Dalian's belt. She tested this extended loop, then, to everyone's astonishment, touched off of the floor, swung, clinging to the belts with all her life, and made it to the other side, stumbling and sitting down, still clutching to the end of the loop. She gave a triumphant look at the three elves, breathing hard. "Our battle plan!" she said with determination.

Endia was the first to cheer, and Zachtia threw the improvised loop as hard as she could so it would swing to be caught by the Yellow Elf. With a deep breath, Endia shut her eyes, got a running start, and jumped!

By now the board and rope were rapidly decaying, and they creaked and groaned dangerously under her weight. She gave a little shriek and, in sudden panic, flung herself onto the other side of the gap and landed hard on the steps. Zachtia scrambled for the belts and managed to catch one as Endia's panic pulsed through the Yellow elf, the momentary flash of bravery and determination subdued by an equally momentary flash of Yellow fear.

"It's okay," Zachtia soothed, rubbing Endia's shoulder with her free hand. "You did it."

"I did it," sniffed the Yellow with a small smile, wiping the tears streaming down her face.

Zachtia waited until the board and noose disappeared, the improvised extensions falling away into her hand. She looked back up at Aldrin and Dalian – who were still standing, a bit stunned, on the other side. "Well, that was our way across," she said to them with an apologetic smile. "You guys'll need to take the next mussum."

The mention of the six-legged transport from common myth elicited a laugh from Endia, and Dalian looked at Aldrin as the noose appeared. He gestured and said with a sardonic smile. "You first."

Chapter 14

Why did he do it?

The deadly fire in Zachtia's eyes had dimmed as they were now on the other side. Endia was still nursing her shoulder and walking close to Aldrin, both of which were behind the Red elf. Zachtia was keeping to herself, eyes boring into Dalian's skull as they climbed the rest of the stairs.

She was not about to ask any more questions. She was a Red Elf. She had asked too much, prodded for information like a child, lost in this fantasy that Aldrin had prodded her into.

Why did he do it?

Why was she still asking that question? She never needed to know the opinion of others before. Her husband's opinions, when he gave them, were a gift, and he saw hers as the same. They were never like this, they knew their duties. It wasn't like they were the chatterbox Greens or Yellows. It didn't feel right to ask questions, and yet during this trip through the mines, she had felt *compelled* to ask questions, to glean more information than just by sight and sound. Was it because she was being influenced by the company she was now keeping? Or was it, more likely, she saw the strategic need for it? To garner information that was understood by the two other races but not hers?

But now the question of Dalian's surprisingly blunt attitude against her repeated again and again in her mind, and it wasn't a strategic question. It was personal. Like that conversation in the field with Aldrin all those days back, when she asked him if he had considered doing the ritual in becoming a Red.

"… So why did you it?" she asked softly, almost not believing the question had finally escaped her lips.

Dalian turned and looked at her, and she continued, "What is with your blunt attitude against me?"

He stared at her with an expression of bemusement mixed with that ever-present sardonic smile. "Well, what would you have done, Lady Red, if you saw one of your soldiers wallowing in self-pity, and the only way to bring him out of it was to strike him across the face?"

"I'd slap the self-pity out of him… yes." Zachtia's eyes narrowed, that fire flashing in them. "And you saw that your position as our guide called for that?"

"Yes, as a matter of fact," he came back evenly. "I've gone through this tower before, you know, but I was either by myself multiple times, or was with two other teams multiple times. You know your strengths and weaknesses as well as Endia's, I don't. Sure, I could have figured out a way to get across that gap. I'd probably get the same method you did. But up until I pushed you…" He stopped, choosing his words carefully. "How much have you contributed to this voyage? Emotional support for Aldrin, I'll grant you that, but what qualities that you have been gifted as a Red have you used for this group's strategic benefit during this voyage, hmm?"

It sounded as if Aldrin was about to say something, but Zachtia held up a hand. "I can speak for myself, Aldrin," she said firmly, eyes fixed on Dalian. Finally, she sighed tiredly. "You're right, I have contributed my name and my compassion, but nothing else. I've asked too many questions, and I'm sorry."

Dalian's eyes softened. "Both are very good qualities," he said softly. "And keep asking those questions, Zachtia, especially with this lot." He nodded, and Zachtia felt Aldrin's hand cautiously grasp her shoulder. She squeezed it with her hand and then looked at Dalian and nodded.

The Black Elf made a sweeping gesture up the stairs into the next corridor. "Shall we continue?" he asked.

Level 17

"Now this one will go very quickly if I remember correctly, and if we don't all panic," assured Dalian, stepping into the hallway.

Zachtia, Aldrin, and Endia followed him from the steps and stopped. This was another nondescript hallway, everything appearing normal and uninteresting… except that in the moments it took for them to come into view of it, the hallway had lengthened about twelve yards. Not only that, but as it had lengthened – not stretched, but developed in length – doors, arches, and hallways for corridors materialized into existence as if they had been grown, the wood paneling coming into existence, then the hinges, then the actual doors themselves. Where there was a curtained archway for a corridor, drapes folded into existence in the openings, and finally the wood itself varnished with that new, waxy, brown color.

The group stayed behind Dalian and waited for him to move. When he didn't, they stood and watched.

After about thirty seconds, the hallway crunched itself to about halfway between the length it was and the length it had become, six doors on either side fading away and two new double-doors taking up similar places on either side. Then, thirty seconds later, they too faded as the original hallway reasserted itself.

"How is it doing that?" asked Endia, awed at the spectacle.

"Look closely at the walls on the middle iteration," answered Dalian.

After about a minute the longest iteration of the hallway came into existence and they all peered at the intricate carvings in the walls. They were embedded in the walls and they looked like pitch-black marble.

"Mica," said Zachtia, her perfect falcon vision making out the detail. "They used Mica stones. That's why the timeline's so fuzzy, why it's lengthening and shortening instead of staying in one spot."

She felt the eyes of everyone in the group on her and her head jerked over and refocused on Aldrin. "What? I've been listening," she retorted.

Dalian chuckled at that. "A lateral deduction, you *are* learning," he said and she made a face at him. "That's what we can tell as well – yes, the Mica carvings are the reason the hallway isn't simply disappearing and reappearing in its other states but lengthening and shortening, as if it's in the same timeline as itself."

"So, how are we going to get through?" asked Endia. "Ride the tide to the other side?"

"Actually, it's not that simple, Endia," answered Dalian, stifling a sincere chuckle at her choice of words. "Our door is at the third iteration, the double doors on the right."

"Wonderful," muttered Zachtia sardonically. "Is it a question of timing or do we run half the time until the doors get there?"

"Timing," replied Dalian approvingly. "You'll switch roles with Aldrin in a moment."

Zachtia was about to retort when she realized that Aldrin had been quiet for most of the journey from the gap. Even through the hallway whose walls suddenly burst open in wide gaps – without any debris – his warnings of caution were softer than expected. She turned to him. "Are you alright?" her voice laced with concern.

"I will be," he said in that soft voice.

"What's wrong?"

The Green Elf had been examining the wall when she had asked her question and now looked at her. "Take a moment and stretch out your mind. What do you sense?"

The answer was immediate, but it was from Endia. "The Purple!" she squeaked, looking down the passage they had come. She looked at Aldrin with a sudden realization on her face. "My sword! I haven't had it since we escaped from the jail!" Her panic was quelled by Aldrin, who held up a hand and made as if patting a satchel at his side. "Don't worry, I brought it with me."

The Yellow smiled and then her eyes went wide. "How big is that thing?!" she cried.

"About – " Aldrin began.

"Apparently big enough," interrupted Zachtia, letting her Red roots show once again. "But you were talking about the Purple. Is he here? What's your plan?"

"He's not here," replied Aldrin after a pause. "But he is still tracking us. That's another question I have – why is he still tracking us?"

By now Zachtia had stretched out her own senses and her brow furrowed with concentration. "That's the same Purple that chased me with his mate." She grunted. "Almost feel honored with being such a prized meal."

"Yeah…" Aldrin looked up towards the ceiling, which in this location was about three feet from his head. "He's not here," he repeated slowly. "He's above us."

"He's in the Bane?" asked Endia, bewildered.

"And has been following us erratically," continued Aldrin. "I noticed his presence earlier, around that part with the gap. He keeps having to backtrack and go alternate routes to get back to directly above us, like his mind has a lock on ours."

"Considering we're the only ones alive down here," sniffed Zachtia, "I'd say you're right."

The matter was set aside for the moment – though not without one or two more looks to the ceiling – as the group waited once again for Dalian to move.

Finally, with an urgent "Go!" Dalian darted forward, followed closely by his charges. Halfway down the corridor, however, one of the double doors opened and *Aldrin* – with the Aldrin with the group looking agape at him – leaned in, looking concerned. "It's that door," the Aldrin said quickly, pointing to the first set of double doors which the group had passed, and then jumped backwards, shutting his door in front of him.

All of them looked at Aldrin, but Dalian was the first to snap out of it. "Of course!" He cried, flinging the door open. "Come on, come on!"

Aldrin, Zachtia, and Endia all followed suit and ran through the door, not daring a second look. After Aldrin stepped through with the girls in front of him, he looked back at the door to find it was gone. The stone wall of the tower had replaced it. "That was... interesting," he said. "I wonder when that will happen."

Zachtia put her hand to her head, "Can anyone explain to me what just happened?" She asked, her voice husky with depleted energy.

"We saw Aldrin," replied Endia in an awed voice. "So, sometime, in the future, we'll come upon a door that he'll lean through and tell us in the past about that door."

Aldrin had to smile as Zachtia groaned and leaned against the wall. Endia's intelligence and quick thinking was always a breath of fresh air for him. He frowned, looking at Dalian. "So that would mean that the door that future me came through would have been higher in the tower."

"But further along in time," responded Dalian, tilting his head. "We don't know how long it's been since future us got there, *and* we might have run into them if we went through that door."

"Gentlemen, please," pleaded the Red elf in their midst. "I'm sweaty, hungry, and very tired. Could we please cut the future-magic debate and rest for a moment?"

There was talking in the far distance along the corridor, but no Goblyn was forthcoming. They chose that moment – for Dalian and Endia rather reluctantly – to sit down and pass out a portion of the rations. They were in a smaller room, most likely the latrine or "pot room" with all the holes posted along the walls, and water pumps in the corners. Thankfully the smell of decay had not carried over in the time iterations of the tower, though there was a continuous loop of unseen water trickling that quelled the appetite.

After eating and a quick rest afterward, they were ready to move again.

Level 23

"What's wrong?" asked Aldrin, tapping Dalian on the shoulder.

The last levels had been scaled without incident. The voices they heard were like those in the "whisper level," except most of the words Aldrin had picked out were orders of laundry. It also turned out that the community pot room was "powered" by a washroom above, the water using gravity to build its pressure for an intricate "flush-out" system. Aldrin would have been delighted to spend a few minutes looking at the plumbing, seeing if he could replicate it, but the girls gently but firmly coaxed him on.

Finally, after another rest in what appeared to be a greenhouse, they had reached the next "interesting" level: Level 23.

"This level we have to be very cautious," Dalian informed him, his voice low, almost a shaky whisper. "This is also one of the levels that makes me shudder."

"That's a first," commented Zachtia in a wry tone, but as quiet as Dalian. "I'm not sure if I've seen you shaken on any of these levels before."

"What's wrong?" Endia repeated Aldrin's question. "What's so shudder-inducing?"

With a chuckle (to calm his nerves, Aldrin guessed,) the Black elf said, "This is the part where we'll meet the Goblyns. And if we're not careful, we might literally *meet* them. I should know." They looked at him expectantly, and he continued, "Two times ago, when I was here, I stayed in a doorway too long and a Goblyn saw me. He rushed out and said – well, you'll get to hear what he said because it's now an integrated part of their timeline."

Aldrin whistled low, eyebrows furrowed. "I really wonder why some places of the tower are like this and some aren't."

"It may be because the time-rift-thing has different branches, and not just like a beam of light," said Endia and all turned to her. "We've been thinking of it like a beam of light streaming in like a window, but maybe it's more like lightning, with the Prophecy Room at the point of origin, and some places are caught in stronger branches."

"So how do we avoid being seen?" asked the Red of the group, bringing them back to the moment. She then grimaced and looked at Dalian, cocking an eyebrow. "If you'll give me a map of all the Goblyns there and where they are, I could give us a plan," she said, her voice not combative but nevertheless level.

"Thank you, Miss Red," said Dalian with an approving grin, some appreciation in his voice as well as some returning smugness. "But I actually have a plan. And it's, uh, simple too. To get to that place we'll be fine, as long as we don't cross anywhere where light falls."

"Where light falls. Underground," intoned Aldrin, blinking. "Do they have, what, a sophisticated lighting system to mimic sunlight?"

"That would be interesting to see," Endia replied with a grin.

A Warrior's Code

"No," Dalian's voice cut through the chatter, hard and back to hesitant. "It's where… I don't know how else to explain it – it's where time has solidified more. The brighter the place is, the more solid the time state is. Clear?"

Blinking, the group fell silent and Endia and Aldrin nodded simultaneously.

The floor wasn't pitch black, as some of the elves of the party feared it would be, but rather a misty light filtered through lamps suspended from the ceiling, Mirror-Glass dispersing it.

The entire level felt like it was underwater. It felt thick, and Endia had to take in a few breaths just to remind herself she was on land. It had a sad, longing sort of feel that being underwater does, except the beauty of the reef was traded in for the fascinating architecture of the Goblyns.

Wherever light was beaming from a door it looked foggy and distorted.

And there were Goblyns. Not quite in reach, not quite in reality, but looking as if they were from the blurry, off-center vision of the corner of your eye. They moved in daily tasks - one Endia immediately took a liking to was a little girl Goblyn taking water to everyone. "It looks like everyone has a job to do here," she whispered.

They passed several doorways, treading carefully around the beams of light emanating from them. They could hear voices, and the Goblyns they saw looked solid and fully visioned.

But there was one archway and beam of light that was unavoidable. The grand room bottlenecked into a corridor, and then to a flight of stairs, but just before the stairs was a grand archway, with the light shining full onto the other wall.

"This is where I was seen," Dalian whispered with an edge of nervousness.

They neared the room. Like most of the other rooms as they got near it, voices started emanating like wisps of audible smoke from the room. They crept ever nearer, and Endia heard Aldrin very softly say, "Map... turning... army..."

"Translating?" she asked in a hoarse whisper, but Dalian shushed her and glared at Aldrin.

They made it to where Dalian could have reached a hand out and bathed it and his arm in the pooling light. Everyone was silent now. Dalian looked over at Aldrin again and signed "Seen-Play"

Aldrin thought he understood and waited, placing a hand on Endia's shoulder to keep her from moving.

Abruptly, they heard a gasp from inside the room, and within a second a slender but well-built Goblyn ran out of the room, dressed in a general's robe with paladins and a gold sash across his chest. He was looking around while yelling in the Goblyn's tongue and Zachtia had to bite her lip to keep from shrieking as he looked straight at the group, looked away – and then he disappeared.

For some reason, they all looked at Aldrin. "I think he said 'We are invaded, I just saw an elf,'" Aldrin translated, giving a wide-eyed look at Dalian.

"Exactly," Dalian said. "Now, wait for about..." he looked up. Aldrin took it he was crunching his numbers. "Now, Endia, cross over."

Endia skittered across the pool of light, and was once again shrouded in darkness.

"Now Zachtia," said Dalian. "Go."

Zachtia obeyed and was soon with Endia.

Aldrin spoke up next, "Now you, Dalian."

Dalian looked at him with a raised eyebrow and Aldrin nodded him on insistently. "Don't be stupid," Dalian warned, but he crossed over anyway.

Aldrin took a deep breath, and stepped into the pool of light, but instead of running across the threshold, he took his time while looking at the room. He memorized every aspect of it: The tall, library-like shelves filled with books and scrolls, the table map that appeared to be a 3D model of the mines in relation to the surface above, the three Goblyns in their military garb, and the one looking directly at him.

It was the same one that had run forward, having looked at the doorway at the most inconvenient time. It now pointed at Aldrin, gasping and Aldrin bolted, almost bowling over Endia in his haste.

The Goblyn then ran out of the room, yelling what Aldrin had translated "We are invaded! I just saw an elf!" before disappearing.

Aldrin looked apologetically at the group, but Dalian was looking at him with a look of curiosity, not anger. "So, who was it," the Black elf whispered, his eyes sparkling in the light from behind Aldrin, "that the Goblyn saw, hm? You or me?"

"We can discuss it farther along," said Zachtia impatiently. "Let's move from this creepy place."

Level 26

They neared yet another passage with rooms, this one brightly lit, when Dalian stopped them and mildly cursed. "I'm sorry, I've lost count," he said. "Ever since we got up those stairs that jiggled, I have been counting down, there's something here we have to be wary of."

"A trap?" asked Endia, remembering what Dalian had said about the Goblyns' love for traps.

"No," said Dalian, nearing one of the rooms but not crossing over. "More of an annoyance..."

Aldrin neared him, but Dalian's hand shot up, arm splayed over his chest. "Wait."

A disgruntled cry came from the room and a frying pan whizzed eye-height through the air from it and clanged into the wall opposite. "There it is," said Dalian, relaxing. "We'll have no more problems in this hallway, continue."

They crossed the other rooms without incident, though Aldrin observed Zachtia hobbling across the light of the four doorways more quickly than before. Apparently, she wanted to be seen no more than Aldrin.

They arrived at the steps, but these were much shorter than the ones that led to the other floors. "This is where it gets dangerous," Dalian reminded those who could remember his explanation on the second floor and Zachtia harrumphed. "I mean it, Zachtia," he said bluntly. "This is where time splits into *three* timelines, like in that Whispers level. We'll have some brief respite on this floor here," he continued, climbing the stairs, the rest of them following, "But then we'll have to be more alert than ever before."

He led them to a large doorway and there was a cacophony of sound emanating from it. "Ready for this?" he asked, and when all the group nodded, he added, "We have to cross over this way to the other side of the Tower, the rest is... blocked off. Move when I say. And try not to eat the food."

His smug smile returned, resurrected by the odd expressions he was receiving from the elves.

With that, they all entered through the door.

The cacophony broadened for their ears and for a moment all the elves new to the tower just stood there, drinking in the sight.

It was a Coliseum, but not one to fight in. This Coliseum, complete with wide open area below and levels held above by humongous, elaborate buttresses, was for eating in. It was a cafeteria!

Food. Without the warning from Dalian, the elves probably would have made for one of the many buffet lines lining the upper level. Now, they just drooled despairingly as they saw rows of slain beast sitting in pots and pans, cooked masterfully with vegetables and doused with sauces. Fountains of wine and water gurgled between each line.

All this Aldrin took in in a moment.

"This isn't fair," Endia whimpered. All of it looked so good.

"We all need to tighten our belts," said Zachtia with a coldness that brought them back to their situation, though she too was licking her lips a moment before. "Let's move on."

Dalian brandished a hand. "Head over to those buttresses," he said, gesturing to a set of four statuesque pillars that lined the stairs that led down to the ground floor. "In the shadows we should be fine. You have to see this."

At this time, the Goblyns in the room had that "corner of your eye" look about them and the elves had to dodge quickly sometimes to keep from bumping – or worse, phasing through – the many blurry bodies that were moving around, chattering. They made it to the cover of the pillars, and at Dalian's insistence they all turned and carefully peered around each of their pillars.

About a moment later, all Goblyns became solid. The indistinct clamor that had been issuing from them now became distinct chatter. But thankfully no one seemed to have noticed the four elves, who were otherwise looking very conspicuous, flattening vertically on their pillars and looking around.

Aldrin wondered if this had been Dalian's plan all along, to get them to a safe place before everything started into motion again. Then again, he too was fascinated with what was going on. Like his superior's thoughts on the Red elves, he had to fight thoughts of the Goblyns being his enemy or opponent, something that was out to get him. He wondered if Endia was having the same trouble with her Yellow paranoia. He watched down below at the many square and round tables set up on the floor below. This also once again gave him a sense on how big the tower really was, as the opposite wall of the room was at least a hundred feet from them. All this travel in the outer passages and hallways had condensed the size of the tower in his mind.

Endia was fascinated by the entire concept of "cafeteria". She could relate a little with the "community table" back in her forest, but *this*: many "community tables" in one room. The food was gotten on the second and third "tiers" of the level, and then brought down to the tables or otherwise eaten around the buttresses.

And they were chatting. Not with angry words, but casual, friendly tones. Laughter and musical lilts of contented voices filtered up to her ears. Endia even spied a couple leaning on the corner wall of the Cafeterium, lost in each other as they kissed and muttered between themselves.

Zachtia wished they would all just disappear so they could continue, but at the same time the Red had a grudging fascination as well. These creatures were a bit of a mystery to her. At the beginning, she had felt a faint connection with them with their love of traps and dislike of "guests" invading their home. Now, to her they had an almost *Green* quality. She looked over at Endia, who by now was looking at Aldrin. When Endia looked back, Zachtia saw a look of wistfulness. The little dear.

And to think that way of a Yellow made her bite her lip. Why was there a war? Why did it have to be this way? She had already made her peace with Aldrin – she even counted him as a brother, and Endia a good friend. But in this isolated tower they were all equals. Outside the tower, once home, would they all be enemies again?

It was at this thought that the scene abruptly changed. All the Goblyns fizzled, as if submerged underwater, then became solid again, in different places. Aldrin gave a cry as a piece of potato whizzed past his ear, and Endia squeaked as a piece of celery clipped her tunic. Zachtia's attention snapped back to the center. The sounds had shifted, still friendly but with a mischievous menace in it, as the whole center of the Cafeterium had become an all-on food fight! Patrons on the upper tiers were shouting encouragement at the opponents at each table, and each table had been aligned on either one side of the wide area, or the other, with a painted line between them. Each side had miniature catapults and hand-held slingshots – this had been premeditated, thought Zachtia instantly – and food was flying everywhere. Pieces of roasted beast, vegetables, and something icy cold and creamy splattered on the buttress and bits of it caught her in the face. She brushed it away and, on a whim, sucked her fingers. It was sweet.

Dalian was laughing as he dodged the food as well from behind his buttress. It was a genuine laugh, he was having fun. As was Aldrin, who Zachtia noted had caught an apple with his hand – like the rock she had flung at him out of fear all those days (weeks?) ago – and had taken a bite out of it before tossing it back.

And suddenly it all changed again, and all smiles disappeared from the elves' faces.

The sounds of laughter and of fun were replaced by the cries of an actual battle. Smears of the iced cream and splatters of vegetables were replaced by the smears and spatters of blood and organs.

Zachtia held her breath as she took in the sight. Tables had been overturned, the occupants either lying dead around them or fighting for their lives, and their opponents drove them hard in full armor, complete with swords, shields, spears, and arrows. Zachtia peered forward with her falcon sight at one said opponent. "Aldrin," she barked abruptly in shock. "They're elves!"

And they were. Graceful and unrelenting, the elves were massacring the Goblyns, and Zachtia felt a pang of guilt rise in her throat like bile. These Goblyns hadn't been fighting, they had been at peace!

Like the Greens. The Greens fought like masters, but they couldn't stand up to the powerful onslaught of the empirical Reds. And like the Goblyns they wanted peace...

She looked over at Aldrin, to find him looking at her. His expression said it all. He was thinking the same thing too. His hands were gripping the rockwork of the buttress and his brows were furrowed in empathetic fury. Then he glanced sideways.

Endia shrieked in terror as Aldrin yanked her out from her shadow and held her in his arms. A Goblyn had been slammed into where she had been standing and now was looking blankly at a broadsword through his chest. Aldrin was gripping Endia, not letting her move or turn to see the Goblyn slump and fall, the tip of the sword raking against the buttress and blood smear down it in the path of the body.

And then, it was all over.

All Goblyns disappeared. All elves disappeared. The buttress kept its engraving from the sword, but the deceased Goblyn was gone, his blood old and black on the pillar.

Endia was crying, and all eyes were on Dalian, who nodded simply and said, "Now we can cross over."

Silently but with a grim eagerness to get out of there, Zachtia and Aldrin, carrying Endia, followed Dalian down the stairs, through the graveyard of dust and wood that was once the friendly and jovial Cafeterium, up the stairs opposite, and through the other doorway.

It was Zachtia who spoke up first. She was immediately in Dalian's face. "Endia could have been killed!" her voice thundered and she glared daggers into Dalian's eyes.

"I know," said the Black elf solemnly. "And I am sorry. I really am," he said in a somewhat petulant voice, looking at Endia who had gotten down from Aldrin and was now rubbing the tears from her eyes. "I was here by myself when I found the alternate route, I didn't remember that bit of the battle. I'm sorry," he repeated this time to Endia. She nodded numbly and Aldrin knelt beside her.

But it wasn't to comfort her, he was in pain and he groaned.

"And didn't I tell you to try not to eat the food?" asked Dalian, cocking an eyebrow. "I imagine that it has retracted itself from your digestive system. Be grateful your body hadn't had more time to absorb it."

Zachtia didn't know about the intricacies of digesting, nor did she care. She did, however, now observe the numbness on her tongue where she had licked the iced cream off her fingers.

Chapter 15

Level 27

The group walked up the stairs leading to the next floor above the Cafeterium. Dalian was in front as always, Zachtia in the middle, and Aldrin was carrying Endia on his back. She had first declined this, saying that she wasn't a child. But then she had sensed the open concern for her from the Green elf as he said, "I know." She let him carry her. Part of her was enjoying the rest she was having from being on her feet, and more than just a part of her enjoyed the intimacy as she clung to him.

And his mind let her know he was enjoying it, though only half as much as she was.

He was the one still walking.

They heard sounds coming from this next level, light shining into a narrow hallway from the open door. "Not again," Endia groaned. She'd had enough of people being slaughtered, especially, now that she thought about the time differences, if those Goblyns dying were the same ones they heard going to school as younglings in the Level of Whispers. "Please tell me there's another way," she said to Dalian.

"No, Miss Yellow," responded the Black Elf, using distancing nouns again. "You'd be faced with an even more grave sight if we were to take the stairs opposite this upcoming door. The battles were very bloody for those who didn't have the high ground."

"High ground doesn't mean anything if you have a spear," Zachtia sniffed. "Or a bow and arrow."

A Warrior's Code

"Indeed," allowed Dalian. "But it's too narrow for two, let alone *four* elves to get through safely. This..." The door was nearly directly left of him and he tapped the wood of the especially made doorway with a knuckle. "This is the safest route. And yet I warn you, know it'll be more dangerous for us personally than that, uh, big food room."

"The Cafetcrium?" asked Endia, naming it on the spot with old words she knew. "You do realize I was almost made a skewered dish."

"Okay, maybe not as dangerous in *that* sense," Dalian agreed. "But there's more of a chance of being seen. Time crosses over more solidly here and we have a much shorter gap between the 'reset' into our time and the other two times."

"Two time jumps now?" asked Zachtia, tilting her head with a frown. "Just once, for once, I'd like this tower to make *sense*."

"Blame the rift," said Dalian flatly. "Don't blame me. Now come on, I'll tell you when to move."

"Could I get down?" asked Endia. "I'm alright now." She clambered down with a grateful smile at Aldrin and they passed through the doorway.

The first thing to strike them was the brightness of the grand room. It was another room that spanned the entirety of the Tower width-wise, but it was all one floor and was almost as bright as real time. Which, as Dalian pointed out, it *was* real time at the moment. He ushered them quickly to a dark spot in the room and not a moment too soon.

That's when the music started. Dalian signed "Music Hall" and Aldrin had no trouble translating, if some understanding. But the music was absolutely beautiful. The room had dimmed slightly and the figures had appeared, transparent but halfway visible. There were about fifty of them, thirty sitting in chairs and listening quietly in one portion of the Hall, while at the other end were the other twenty. Most of the twenty were also sitting, and each had in hand an instrument, though the two in the back had drumsticks for their bells and drums. Some of the instruments Aldrin could place like the lute, the trumpet, the harp, the flute, but there were quite a few variations on these that he could only guess at.

He had just gotten into the music, when the scene changed again. Endia pressed her face hard into the side of his abdomen and whimpered. It was once again the invasion of the elves.

Except this time, the elves were *losing* the fight, at least in this room. Aldrin watched, both with fascination and to keep his mind occupied and from thinking about his own war. The same Goblyns, older now, who were playing their instruments in the first iteration, were using their instruments as weapons! Or else had picked up the weapon of a fallen elf and was using that. He was following one particular female Goblyn who had what looked to be a shoulder-mounted lute played with a flat bow of sorts as she deftly plowed the bow into the uncovered eye of her opponent and then slammed the shoulder-lute into his face.

And then all disappeared.

"Let's watch it a few times," Dalian said quietly. "So we know how much time we have."

It was only five seconds before the cycle repeated. Exact same song, exact same battle, silence... they watched it for three more iterations and Endia – who watched it all on the last one, observed that there was a time where some of the audience gasped and pointed at the floor near the doorway.

Finally, an instant after they had disappeared, Dalian spat "Move, *move!*" and they all sprinted for the opposite door. Right before they reached the door, however, Endia gave a cry as she tripped over air. Aldrin's boots screeched on the smooth floor as he halted and ran back over to her.

The scene of the music hall was back but not fully visible and Aldrin hauled Endia to her feet and carried her like a sack of potatoes through the doorway, noticing the gasps of the audience but not daring to stop. He shot out of the room and set Endia down between them.

"Maybe I -" he began.

"- *should* carry me," said Endia in a pouting tone. "Sorry everyone."

"Are you alright?" asked Zachtia concernedly. "You tripped over the stand of one of those bigger stringed instruments."

"And solved one of our mysteries," added Dalian, and Endia looked up at him. "We weren't sure why the Goblyns were pointing there and gasping, now we know – or I know until I get back to the encampment to tell everyone." He pursed his lips, probably having the same thought as Aldrin. "If there's anyone left when I get back. Come on, 20 more levels to go."

Level 35

There was the sound of a door opening and closing. The group had climbed the flight of stairs and Zachtia demanded a rest. "It's not the journey," she said with a tired grin. "It's the payload."

Aldrin wasn't listening. They were in a wider passage, like a broad hallway, with steps at the far end leading sharply up. He was listening to the creaking of the door in the middle of five lining the opposite wall. He neared it and examined it. It was a regular door, but the doorway had intricate carvings of silver and Mica. Excited, he watched as it opened, and the room beyond was very dark, having a table and two chairs. Then it closed about ten seconds afterwards, reopening in five, revealing a brightly lit room, filled with Goblyn children. One of them looked at him and waved, babbling in their language. Before the adult in the corner had time to look up from her scroll to see Aldrin, the door had closed.

The third time it opened, it revealed exactly what he was hoping it would: the hallway where they were before on Level 17. He wanted to say something different, just to see what it would do, how it would affect the timeline. But, with the wisdom of a Green and with an inward groan, he stuck his head through the door and said quickly, "It's that door." He pointed to the first set of double doors which the group had passed, and then jumped backwards, shutting his door in front of him. With a deep breath, he turned to face the group to find everyone staring at him. "Now we know," he said, the door behind him now open and bathing him in sunlight. He was pulled by Dalian away from the door as it closed on whatever was making a screeching noise. He looked at Dalian and tilted his head, "Back there, you said 'of course' before leading us through the wrong door, which turned out to be the right door. Why's that?"

"Because, for whatever reason it opens and shuts, maybe because of the Mica-Silver mix, or because of a spring mechanism," Dalian explained softly, "That door never opens on the same area twice. We watched it, we observed it, but it never has. Unlike the rest of the tower, it's completely random."

Endia was watching the door now, jumping as she heard a *squawk-THUD* as apparently someone was making dinner. "Could we go?" she asked. "Rest somewhere else?"

"Thanks for clarifying," came Zachtia's tired reply. "Maybe somewhere that isn't weird."

Zachtia was helped to her feet by Aldrin and they all started for the far stairway. Endia was passing the door when she stopped and stared through it. "Aldrin?" she called to the Green near her, not looking away from the door.

What she saw was the ground floor of the Tower with three figures standing and looking around. They all wore satin clothing, with black pants, strange silver calf-boots, and the same kind of top. But each shirt was a different color, and each was a totally different being. The one male in the green shirt was definitely an elf, about the same height as Aldrin with nice brown hair. The second male was in blue and he had rounded ears, and he was short and stocky, as if someone had stretched him widthwise. The girl – the girl who was looking directly at her – was in red. What was most startling about her was her skin color was green! She had black hair in a ponytail, and was about the same height as Endia herself. "GeeAyy!" the green girl cried, pointing at Endia with a look of shock.

And the door closed once again.

Endia hurried to join the others. Aldrin was beckoning to her. "What'd you see?" he asked curiously.

"Three figures..." She explained their description and then looked around at the rest of them. "The elf looked okay, but the others – they didn't feel real; like they weren't supposed to be there." She shrugged helplessly and jumped when two voices walked down the stairs in front of them, chatting softly.

Dalian nodded, though his focus was up the stairs. "This upcoming level," he said softly "It's the 'everything drops' floor. We're almost at the Throne Room and then the Prophecy Room and this will bypass eleven of the floors."

"That sounds nice," muttered Zachtia, then she frowned and she looked up at the Black Elf. "If I recall, though, this is where we'll have as much room as fish caught in a net."

Dalian nodded. "Correct. We'll come to that soon." He led the way up the small staircase and through a small door. Beyond the small door was a vast, circular chamber. It felt to Aldrin like the defunct lookout-lighthouse in the center of the Four Towers Library, with a solid cement structure taking the bulk of the room, with a thin staircase spiraling up on the outside of it. They all followed the staircase skyward with their eyes. There were branches off of the inner round tower leading to the separate floors and they could just make out an arched opening in the structure. This contained a massive bell.

"That's where we will have to be," Dalian explained, pursing his lips, "When everything drops. It may look peaceful enough down here," he looked at Zachtia, anticipating her question, "But that's because most of this part isn't part of that timeline. And we can't just run across the bridge either." He looked solemn and Aldrin felt a pang of pain from him.

"Your group found that out personally," the Green said softly. "I'm sorry."

"Sorry won't change anything," said Dalian, his frown deepening in concentration. "This is where I think we need Zachtia's skills." He turned to her and she blinked. "See, I was with a group of highly acrobatic and flexible Black Elves. Now we're standing here with *one* Black Elf, one Green Elf, a Yellow, and a pregnant Red. My own group's choreography is useless."

Anything else he was going to say was suddenly cut off as a chunk of debris – which looked very much like one of the bridges above – came crashing into the staircase, splintering the wood. Aldrin immediately was in front of Endia and the Yellow shrieked with terror as a body of a Goblyn followed a split second later, spattering into the stone and wood of the wreckage with a gut-wrenching *splat.*

The elves stood there looking at the entire scene until it disappeared, and the staircase reverted to normal. Dalian took a deep breath and let it out. "That'd be our cue to start running up the stairs," he said. "We'll have just enough time to get there and get settled before things start happening."

Zachtia nodded, concentrating. She peered up at the bell tower with her falcon vision. "Describe the floor of that inner chamber," she said softly.

"About five feet in diameter," explained Dalian, "With a large, thick grate covering the hole. That structure is hollow so the sound will echo downwards into more of the Tower."

"Hm..." the Red closed her eyes. "Will the bell or the grate move?" she further questioned.

"No, they'll stay in place," further answered Dalian. "Though the entire structure will shake several times and the bell will sound once or twice."

Again the Red nodded, eyes still closed. She motioned to Endia. "Come on up here."

A Warrior's Code

Endia owlishly walked over to the Red and Zachtia lifted her and set her to where she was very lightly sitting on the baby bump of the Red's belly. "Right," Zachtia said, smiling a little. "Dalian, come over and see how tightly you can get up behind us – with your back facing us."

The Black, with a bemused grin, stood with his back against Zachtia's, bracing with his feet so she had to dig her toes into the floor to keep from toppling over.

"Very well," Zachtia grunted. She turned to Aldrin. "... actually, Aldrin, you come up behind me and wrap your arms around me and Endia." She cocked an eyebrow. "Preferably loose enough you don't suffocate me," she added.

Aldrin took Dalian's place, with Dalian shrugging gamely, and carefully wedged himself at Zachtia's back and wrapped his arms around her and Endia.

"That'll do, brother," Zachtia commented with a grunt. "Dalian, you'll be in front, facing outwards."

"I *keep* facing outwards," complained Dalian.

"Because you're not a brother," Zachtia replied flatly, eliciting a giggle from Endia. "Besides, you can watch out for any debris that might fly up or down." She fell silent for a moment and then put Endia down. "Right," she said finally, "Does everyone know-"

The debris crashed again and the body fell.

Dalian interrupted quickly, "Hope everyone does, let's go!"

Aldrin caught up Endia in his arms and followed behind Zachtia, making sure the Red wouldn't fall or lose pace. He grimaced as they neared the bloody wreckage but it dissolved into nothingness as they neared it. Without any more words, they climbed the spiral staircase up and up, passing up bridges that led to other floors. He wondered why Dalian preferred such a dangerous shortcut over just going across those bridges, but then he supposed the alternatives might be just as dangerous with the three timelines playing out.

They neared the top. Zachtia's breath was coming in steady gulps and her pace slowed. She gritted her teeth and pushed through, even though her vision went blurry. She wasn't about to give up now. For her husband's sake. For her baby's. For the little family – and Dalian – she had acquired on this weird journey.

The bell tower had a small railing around it which was quickly becoming more and more eroded as they finally leveled off into the chamber. Dalian took his spot, bracing against the pillars of the archway while Aldrin passed Endia to Zachtia. Aldrin just had time to wrap his arms around the two ladies and dig in his heels when the bridge in front of them abruptly exploded.

All the elves jumped at this as the rocks scattered and specs of it came flying and pelted Dalian's body. "Eeurgh," he grunted out painfully. Most of it had bounced harmlessly off of his rugged black uniform, but the stuff that had caught his face and hands hurt. "You sure I can't turn around?" he asked reproachfully to Zachtia.

The Red didn't answer as another bridge, this one leading to the floor below, also exploded, but now Aldrin caught sight of a large, black, round object rocketing skyward. The cannon ball wasn't something he had seen before but he had read about the destructive capabilities of one at high speed.

The tower shook and he had to regain his footing. He also now saw why he was the one holding Zachtia. With Endia in her arms she was very top-heavy and was using Aldrin for support.

He watched as another cannonball shot up and embedded itself in the wall a few feet to the left of them. He felt Endia squeeze into Zachtia's chest in Yellow terror and the Green tried to comfort her by lifting one arm and stroking her hair. "It'll be over soon – Dalian!" he called in a yelp as the Black suddenly put a foot out and tilted forward!

Only to be met with the bridge, new and undamaged. The Black elf looked cheekily at the stunned group and then his expression turned serious. "I was counting in my head," he said. "Come on, before it starts again."

Chapter 16

Level 46

Zachtia wanted a rest and yet wanted to still see what was ahead. Dalian hadn't gotten to this part in his explanation, and yet this was Level 46, one level below the level with the Prophecy Room. The Black elf in front of her was now treading slowly up the stairs. Perhaps he was tired, or maybe he was being more cautious.

The latter worried her. For one thing, no one had spoken a word since the bell tower. Dalian usually gave a brief explanation of each floor, so to now have him absolutely silent... "Are you going to explain this next level?" she whispered up to him almost inaudibly.

He turned to her with his finger on his lips. "Throne Room," he mouthed.

Throne room? That would make sense, Zachtia realized. After the common folk, the soldiers, and the generals, the king would logically be at the top of his kingdom. She had forgotten the explanation of the Tower from all those floors below; from a few days ago.

Dalian had gotten to almost the top of the stairs. He was crouching now, looking up at the hallway. He breathed out a sigh. "Good," he whispered. "They just left." He motioned to the others and said, "We're safe for a few minutes. We need to get through this hall. Come on."

Thinking that she hadn't been "come on"ed so much since her courtship period with Dalian, the Red followed with thinned lips.

They came into a hallway that was larger than the many they had crossed through on this journey. Pillars lined the walls on either side, with blue tinted light streaming from the ceiling onto each of them.

"Now that is very pretty," said Endia in a hushed whisper. "Fit for a king."

Dalian didn't say a word but jabbed with two fingers pointed at the far end of the hall. In Bacht sign language that meant "hurry yourself up", though Zachtia had heard it explained in stronger terms.

They hurried down the long hallway, with the Yellow and Green giving many a glance to the intricate designs on the walls. Walls with lumens and onyx stones dancing in beautiful circles and figures. It was yet another floor that Aldrin wished he could stay in longer, just to stare at the beauty.

They also noted the moss underneath their feet. It had grown a lot in the years, but in the light, they could see that each sprout of moss was topped with red. Maybe a natural phenomenon, Aldrin guessed, like those trees that "bled" red sap when cut into.

Everyone also felt that feeling of being watched. As if the ghosts of the past weren't really gone, but lurking in the shadows, watching them invade their home. As if this weren't just haunted by time rifts, but the souls of the dead guarding their fallen land.

On top of all this, the room certainly felt like the end to a long journey.

But they knew they weren't through yet.

Dalian ushered them through the door. Literally, as Zachtia now saw that the doors weren't open but had a gaping hole in the center of them. He then instructed them silently to take separate pillars in the room and wait.

Zachtia took one on the right, down one from the door. Now that she wasn't being pulled along by a sense of dread that someone was chasing them, she could look about the room.

This was a room made entirely out of stone. Even the throne, which was a hollowed-out oval with rotted-out cushions on the side and seat, had been carefully carved from the same stone the back wall had been. The pillars were the same as the hallway and the red-tipped moss was here too. The thing that struck her about this long, wide room was how it was lit. There was a strip in the center of the ceiling traveling from front to back, curving skyward in an arch-like fashion, that was made of lumen crystal. Not raw, unprocessed lumen that Zachtia also spotted in lines glowing in the pillars, but lumen that looked like it had been ground into that fine powder like they found in the garden labyrinth and then pressed or glued firmly into the ceiling so it glowed like an iridescent wave of water.

She was staring at this, almost as enraptured in the beauty of it as Aldrin was, when the room came alive. Or rather, the first iteration of the ripple of time started and there were Goblyns standing at the base of the steps to the throne.

In the center of the hollowed-out oval that was his throne was the king. It immediately struck Zachtia that this was a king that could lead men into war, even sitting down he looked like a mountain of a man, or Goblyn, with a chest and bare arms so bulky they could have been made of the same stone as the room. The ringlet he wore on his head was curiously made of lumen as well, and it glowed dimly in the shadows. He was leaning to one side as if bored as the Goblyns talked to him in their language. Zachtia glanced over at Aldrin to find him listening intently. He was probably translating again, getting more out of the conversation than she was.

Finally, the king stood up and cut through the chatter with his own words. It surprised Zachtia to hear a tenor voice ring out of that elephantine being. He sounded much younger than he looked. There was a word repeated by him that she had heard all the way down in the Whispers level and Aldrin had explained to her in one of their stops: Guardian. Maybe he was telling them they were the guardians of the city? Or he was their guardian? She didn't know and for once wished she had Aldrin's ear for languages.

Like many of the other change in scenes, this one was abrupt. A secondary timeline, once again before the Blues had invaded, but now the king was alone with one other. Zachtia immediately guessed wife or concubine. She was dressed in the same armored kilt and vest combination he had, but her ringlet was of ordinary silver. He was talking to her, and it struck Zachtia that he sounded troubled; despairing, as if he were going into a battle he knew he wouldn't win. The Goblyn female curled herself onto him –

And was suddenly lying on the floor, a piece of smoldering charcoal. The scene had changed quicker than the Red had anticipated and she had to bite down on her lips so she wouldn't cry out in fear or in anger.

It was the invasion of the Blues. One Blue was standing in the center with his hands aglow with blue light that sparkled up and down his designs. From the armor and hair, Zachtia could only deduce this was a very high up commander... if not the Emperor himself.

The king of the Goblyns was being held down by three elven guards, who were not surprisingly having trouble keeping him down.

He was shaking with rage and grief, eyes darting to the blackened form of his wife.

Burnt blackened form.

Zachtia looked at Aldrin to find him turned away from the scene, hugging himself, and hand over his mouth, looking as if he were about to throw up. His eyes were squeezed shut; he was fighting himself and his memories and her heart went out to him. If the roles had been reversed and it'd had been her who found her mate in a smoldering heap, she would probably be in a worse situation.

Another roar came from the Goblyn and she whipped her head forward, seeing the king charge forward, having thrown off the elves holding him down, his hands outwards about to tear the invader to pieces.

All of a sudden, the Blue lifted his hands, and sparks of blue lightning shot from them, catching the Goblyn in the face. Stunned, the Goblyn dropped. Coming nearer, the elf finished the job, placing his hand on the head of the king and letting loose another volley point-blank.

The king's body fell next to his wife's.

Zachtia heard a sob and looked across the hall to see Endia with horrified tears streaming down her face, a hand cupped over her own mouth, her whole body in a sympathetic crouch as if she wanted to run forward and help.

The armored elf and his entourage – those who were still conscious, several had been either knocked out or were dead – looked around for the origins of the sob, most of them even looking at the corpse of the Goblyn female.

And then all disappeared.

Zachtia saw Dalian start to move and swiftly moved to Aldrin, shaking his shoulder. "It's over," she said urgently. "Let's go."

With a numb nod and an audible swallow, Aldrin followed behind her as the Red ran to the door Dalian was now holding open up a few stairs behind the pillars the Black elf and Endia had been standing behind.

Aldrin stopped to pick up Endia. Unlike him, the poor woman had actually lost what lunch she had had on the smooth stone floor. He picked her up and held her in his arms with her head on his chest as he was ushered through the door. "I'm so sorry," he said in Endia's ear. "It's been so rough for you this trip, hasn't it?"

"N-next one," replied the Yellow in a choking voice, "No more towers or caves. Or Goblyns. Or time rifts. Or old ration bars."

"I think I can promise that," he said and stroked her hair as he sank to a sitting position with his back against the wall nearest the door.

Level 47

"What was it that was said?" asked Zachtia for the second time. The first time she had asked it, she hadn't realized that the world had temporarily had no grip on the attention of Aldrin. When he didn't answer, she looked and focused on the two sitting exhausted against the wall; Aldrin supporting Endia in his left arm, across his lap. He had pulled a piece of semi-clean cloth from his displaced bag and was cleaning off whatever sick was left on her face.

She had to constantly remind herself Endia wasn't a child. She was a woman in her 60's - quite young, but still marrying age. Aldrin hadn't wanted anything to do with her when they first met her at the table with Endia staring at him with those expressive, bold eyes. Now, with the Yellow laying across his lap and he cleaning her off, Zachtia could see a warmth in his eyes. But she could also see a battle, she could sense it, he still had a deep loyalty to his dead wife and children. She thought about how she would feel if she were tempted to love again if Dairlo died. She pushed the thought away. He *was* alive. She *would* see him again.

Aldrin finally turned to her at the question, putting the dirtied cloth away. "With the meeting with the consultants," he began, "It sounded as if they were giving warnings about the coming invasion. The king then said something about the Guardian saying that all would come out to good. The second meeting, the one with his, uh, wife, was he felt helpless. 'Who am I gambling?' was one phrase he used." The Green settled into thoughtful silence.

"Is everyone ready to move on?" asked Dalian, moving to the bottom of the stairs. "We're almost to the Prophecy Room. We just need get through Scholar's Hall."

Another room he hadn't told them about, Zachtia mused. "Dare I ask what fresh horrors await us there?" she asked. She knew full well it was a very Green question, but she made sure to keep it in a perfectly sarcastic Red tone, she wasn't in the mood for mockery.

"Oh, you can," said Dalian with a fresh tone of snark, but then he became a little more serious as he said, "Not as bad as you've had to go through. Two Goblyns dead, just librarians."

He caught a glare from Aldrin and he pursed his lips. "Okay, fine. Two dead, maybe three, all librarians, the bloodkin of the

Green Tribe of the elves, peace be with them." He tilted his head at the Green elf. "Happy?"

"Aldrin, are you sure he wasn't a Red?" asked Zachtia with a tight smile. "Because that is some wicked Red snark and sarcasm there."

The Black elf rolled his eyes. "Now that we've gotten that out of the way, is everyone ready to move on?" he repeated.

All the troop nodded and Endia got up from Aldrin's lap with a grateful smile. Zachtia wanted to say something to Aldrin, give him a nudge. But Dalian was already walking up the steps and besides, her nudging too hard might send him on the wrong road.

He thought through so much. He would have to think this through too.

Shaking her head, she hurried into step with Dalian up the steps, noting at once the darkness thickening like a fog around them. She wondered what Aldrin would make of it.

Aldrin followed Endia up the blackening staircase, noting with some curiosity that the underwater feeling was back in full force, and the light that streamed in from the top of the steps was muggy, like looking at sunlight through drapes. When he finally got up to the top of the steps, he forgot what the danger was for a moment and instead gawked in awestruck, childlike delight.

The ceiling was barely a foot from his head, and that was at the highest point. There were three "tunnels" branching off from the brief joining of the room leading to the stairwell, each making lazy arches before leveling off into straight cabinets about knee high.

And all three of them – or at least the center one, Aldrin assumed the other three were like it – were filled to overflowing with scrolls, papers, maps, charts, and books. The Goblyn version of a book was very similar to the elven one, with two covers and a binding, but each looked custom made with its own leather, its own paper, and its own binding.

The three tunnels were also bustling with activity. Aldrin felt a hand push him to the wall and he snapped out of his reverie. Dalian was right, he knew. There was no sense in letting the robed Goblyns, walking to and fro, picking up books, writing in their own, and comparing things to each other, see him and have a panic attack. He also deduced that this was one of those areas that the amount of light translated to the amount of visibility or clarity the timeline had.

Part of him wanted to move on but part of him wanted to stay here. There was something about libraries that always felt like coming home. Like the Four Towers Library. Its soothing atmosphere helped him rise from his depression-drenched state and move on with life.

He looked over at Dalian and nodded. "Thank you," he mouthed.

Dalian signed "You're welcome." and then "Watch".

Aldrin did watch. He also listened. Now that he knew how most of the words were pronounced and how they sounded coming off the Goblyn tongue, each sentence held meaning. The Scribes were writing down what sounded to be predictions. He could also see that one by one and with reverence, each of them had some time or another gone into the Prophecy room during this time. The Prophecy room, he also saw, was at the far end of the hall, through a wide double-door that looked heavy and, until each time they opened it, sealed. One of them, a younger one, walked over to his elder sheepishly after coming out of the Room and had asked which mirror to believe.

"The center one, this time," his elder had explained in a low whisper. "It'll be changed again by tomorrow evening."

After translating, Aldrin found that very interesting. Was it simply security protocol to move the mirrors around so that only the ones "in the know" would know which one was right? Was it tradition? Then again...

A thought struck him but he didn't have time to dwell on it as the mood abruptly altered. Elves, three of them, the one in the lead being the Emperor or admiral Blue, were going down the center tunnel, leaving two of the scholars dead in their wake. The last one, the youngest now older by several years, was pounding on the door to the Prophecy Room. He kept crying out "Guardian! Guardian, help! Help please! Guardian!" as the elves drew steadily nearer.

And without warning, the doors both opened. They opened outwards into the Prophecy Room, and the young Goblyn fell flat on his face.

Aldrin saw who had opened the door. He wished he had Zachtia's perfect falcon vision to make out details.

It was a much older Goblyn, with a shock of white hair that curled down in a monk's crown, and he sported impressive side-whiskers that came down to his collarbone. "Come inside, lad," he said calmly, his nasally but oddly warm voice nearly as quiet as the scholar's hushed whisper. "They won't hurt you anymore." He looked up at the stunned group. "Wasn't foretold," he said in a louder, more determined tone.

Silence giving way to a derisive growl, the lead Blue gestured impatiently and his two men spurted forward. The younger Goblyn barely had the time to scuttle into the room before the elves were upon them both.

A Warrior's Code

But Aldrin blinked and they were suddenly on the floor with the tops of their heads resting beside them. He looked at the old Goblyn – the Guardian – to find he was holding a sword with a blade almost longer than his arm and the blade was now bloodied. "No, wasn't foretold, wasn't foretold," he muttered, gazing with a look of steel at the Blue. "Only one will enter. You."

With this, he backed away from the door, letting the sword scrape on the ground in his wake.

The three elves of the Present watched as the Blue walked into the room and a split second later walked back out. It appeared as if he had simply inverted, having walked back out at the same distance as he walked in. Time had stopped when he was in the room, Aldrin realized eagerly.

"We won't be needing you anymore," the Blue elf said in his own tongue to the Guardian, and brought the sword down on the old creature. To everyone's astonishment, the sword simply passed right through the Guardian, as if he were a ghost. However, the Guardian proved real enough as with a disgusted grunt, he reached up and smacked the forehead of the elf with his palm. "Idiot," he said, speaking in his own language, "Your time's done here. You will leave now and you will not come back."

Whether or not the Blue understood him, there seemed to be an understanding between them at that moment. "Very well," the elf said. "I will go. Everything that I have set out to do has been done. I'd advise you to not walk out of your chambers, Guardian," he furthered, sheathing his sword. "You might not like what you see."

He turned to leave, and Aldrin couldn't mistake the evil grin on his face. The Green elf wanted to put his fist into it, the elves had no right in disturbing this peaceful land. What harm had these people done the elves?

The Goblyn watched him go and shook his head. "I know," he said softly, making Aldrin wonder what the elder had actually understood. "I know everyone is gone. It was foretold, you see." He straightened up and sighed as the elf disappeared into shadow. "But I will be here. I'll always be here."

He turned and Aldrin felt his eyes impossibly on him. "Won't I?" he asked softly, before disappearing.

The doors opened and the muggy light streamed in from the room. The elves of the present heard the Guardian's voice snap in Common Elvish, "Come on! Come on, before it starts again."

Aldrin was the first in line this time, catching a ready Endia up in his arms, Zachtia followed panting, and Dalian leisurely jogged up behind.

They entered the room just before they heard the bustle of commotion outside the door. "Don't be worriesome," the Goblyn said, his words thick with the rolling r's of the Goblyn accent. "The revolutions of time have no effect here. Even my time spended in there will go on without me."

The room looked like the inside of a vacant turtle shell, the very brickwork ribbed as if waves had slowly etched them away. The light was warm and welcoming here, and the room was quiet, as even the rustling from outside sounded muffled and damp. The foreboding yet quaint archway at the end of the short room led to a brief hall and to a smaller room: the Prophecy Room.

Zachtia started to sit down, groaning, but the Goblyn was immediately at her side. "Oh no, guests never sit on the stone-cold floor," he said. "Have my chair." He pointed to a chair in the corner beside a small bed. "Not much for comfort for the eons,'" he said. And then he straightened with a gleaming smile. "And yet no time at all." He paused and looked around. Zachtia still hadn't taken the chair, though she had moved to it, and Aldrin and Endia were staring as if they were seeing a ghost. "Did I say something *wrong*?" asked the elder plaintively. "Or did I say something out of tense? Elvish always gives my tongue cramps, it's not built for it."

Zachtia finally sat down, figuring that it wouldn't disappear on her. "Why weren't we informed of this one?" she asked Dalian, scowling. "Or were you setting us up for another big surprise?"

"I'm afraid it's simply more complicated, my dear," the Guardian responded. He slowly walked over to her and sat down on the bed. "But I'm afraid I'll have to tell you momentarily. I'm feeling the centuries coming upon me like a rockalanche." He harrumphed as he leaned back and closed his eyes. "Not that any of you have experienced one... yet."

He suddenly slid sideways onto the bed and Zachtia leaned back against her seat, horrified. "He's stopped breathing," she gasped.

Before she could say anything else, however, he sat up in a blur of motion. Then, in a timeframe of two seconds and in a blur of almost invisible motion, his body was whirled around the room in motions of walking, talking, leaning, sitting, lying, and finally he appeared fully visible again, walking out of the brief hallway to the Prophecy Room.

With his hair a greasy brown, and shorter side-whiskers, he looked younger. He was reading a scroll and muttering in Goblyn, "Laph my dear, I always get the feeling I've read this paragraph before." He spied the elves and the scroll dropped from his hand and he assumed a battle crouch. "Elves! Here? In this sacred place, it's been foretold but not as far flung a time as..." He stopped. His tensed muscles relaxed and he gathered up the scroll from the floor. "My apologies," he said, going back to Common, "It takes a few seconds for everything to resettle." He tossed the scroll onto the bed. "It happens every three hours now," he muttered. "Shorter time-length." He looked with sharp, hyper eyes at Aldrin. "I've wondered if I will simply start dying at a rate I can't go back to living again, so instead of living eternally I'll die eternally. But let's not talk about me, guests!" He scuttled over and wrung Dalian's hand while shaking it. "I haven't had guests since your people came here, Dalian. It's good to lay back eyes on you, yes." He looked over at Aldrin and then Endia, still grasping Dalian's hand. "Who are your new friends? I've never heard their names for some reason – you had a question!" He was jumping from subject to subject like a monkey through a forest as he crossed over to Zachtia and knelt down. "Yes, it's all coming back to me, I told Dalian and his group to not mention me to anyone – which I hold you all to as well,"

He grinned and Zachtia involuntarily shuttered as he showed his rows of two-pronged needle-like teeth. Seeing this, he went back to a closed-mouth grin. "And now you're having another question, go on, ask it."

"Why do you have to be creepy?" asked Zachtia, blinking.

"No, that's not the one, hm." The Goblyn looked over at the other elves and his eyes fell on Endia. "Ah, *wr*ong woman. Can't blame me you all look alike."

Dalian snorted and had to turn away, his face in his palm.

Endia asked, "What happened back there?" She pointed to the bed. "You died an old Goblyn and then it was as if all your personal time was run backward real fast, and now you're here."

"In a way, that's exactly what happened," replied the Goblyn, standing up and backing up a little from the group to garner all their attentions. "I never die, but I do frequently nowadays." His lower lip puckered in a Goblyn pout. "Then I regress into a previous generation of myself. Nice in concept, gets boring the eonth time acircle."

"Regress into a previous generation," Aldrin echoed thoughtfully. "So, you regenerate?"

The Goblyn smiled. "That has a nice ding to it."

"This all sounds very exciting and miles over my head," interjected the Red sitting in the chair. "But I thought this entire journey was so we could visit the Prophecy Room."

The Goblyn – who was now slightly older and grayer by this time – straightened and nodded. "Yes, I know that is part of your destiny here," he said softly. "If I remember correctly, it should be the Green who goes first. If you all go in at the same time, the mirrors would reflect your group future, not your personal."

"Isn't that a good thing?" asked Endia. "Why can't we do that?"

"Because one of the rules of the Room is that..." The Guardian stopped and then tilted his head. "Well, look at that," he said, and everyone glanced at the corner of the room he seemed to be gazing at. They realized afterwards that he was seeing something in his own mind. "Well," he said in a more complacent tone, sitting on the bed. "I see no reason why all of you couldn't go in after your individual trips."

It was through a two-out-of-three toss of a coin that Aldrin was selected to go first, to the victorious annoyance of the Guardian. "I'd told you he'd be first," said the Goblyn. "Why doubt my word?"

"You did change your mind about the rules," Zachtia said flatly, watching Aldrin go.

The Goblyn fumed for a moment, but then brightened. "True, you know that's something I hadn't foreseen, it's a little detail," he said in his regular voice. He looked at Dalian. "Speaking of little details," he said to the Black Elf, who was now sitting in the chair, "Are you doing healthy, Dalian?"

Zachtia looked at their guide. Although he hadn't shown any signs of it during the trip, now they were at rest and she could see the signs of tiredness in his face and body language. His shoulders were slightly stooped as he was slumped forward, and the color around his eyes were a shade darker. "Dalian, are you alright?" She repeated the Goblyn's question, alarmed.

"I'm fine," he said, giving her his regular smart-aleck smirk. "Why wouldn't I be?"

Endia was sitting beside Zachtia, leaning against her. "Because you're as exhausted as we are," she murmured. "I'm younger than all of you and I'm still exhausted."

Dalian nodded a little too complacently. "Yes, that could be it," he said.

Zachtia felt that he was hiding something even now. She bit her tongue in frustration. "Dalian," she muttered, but said nothing more. He wasn't her husband. She couldn't coax the truth out of him.

Aldrin walked back into the room from the Prophecy Room. He had a very somber expression on his face as he said, "Your turn, Endia."

Endia nodded and got up. She paled a little when she reached the threshold of the hallway, but she pressed on, disappearing out of sight.

"Trouble?" Asked Zachtia softly to Aldrin.

"Shh!" warned the Guardian with two fingers to his lips. "You can't discuss it, at least not in here. You'll find out soon enough."

The Red groaned.

In about five minutes, the Yellow returned. Her eyes were glistening, and she went straight to Aldrin leaning against the wall, wrapping her arms around his waist and clutching him tight, as if by releasing him he'd fade away forever.

"My lady Red," said the Goblyn in a soft voice, "I think it's your turn."

Setting her teeth, Zachtia made her way to the arch of the hallway. Taking a deep breath as if preparing for a high-dive, she went in.

The further she went along the hallway, the smoother and farther apart the waves in the ceiling were, until she finally reached the Prophecy Room.

It wasn't a large room. Only one or two elves could stand abreast of each other after stepping from the hallway to the circular room. Most of the room was taken up by elf-height, flat cuttings of Onyx stone.

And Mica stone, she reminded herself.

As soon as she walked to where she was in the center of the room with the half circle of the five mirrors was around her, the images on the stones became clear. Each time iteration lasted around ten seconds, though that was enough for her for some of them:

The far-left mirror had her being torn to pieces by the Purple Elf, the contents and life in her womb spilling out like an upended bowl. She nearly threw up as she watched and was eager to move on.

The center-left mirror depicted her and Endia walking into Zachtia's home in Scarlesh. She watched eagerly as they walked in and saw a figure in white, but the face was shielded from her sight. No matter how many times it repeated, she couldn't discern the face.

In the center one, she saw herself kneeling and sobbing over Endia, whose body was broken in the same way the Red's had been in the first iteration. She shuddered and wondered how likely two-out-of-three deaths could be. But she knew she was missing something.

The center-right mirror had something almost as gag-worthy as the first: it depicted her intimately kissing the Purple elf while Endia watched in horror.

Finally, the far-right one also showed them walking into the house of Dairlo and Zachtia, however there was no white figure to greet them. Instead it was Dairlo, who grasped his wife in a hug and kissed her more passionately than he ever had.

Zachtia finally realized what was missing in all iterations:

Aldrin. Aldrin wasn't in any of them.

That was why he was so somber coming out of the Prophecy Room. That's why Endia was now clutching at him for fear of him vanishing.

She walked back out of the room after viewing the moving pictures of the mirrors several times. She found Aldrin had taken up her spot on the bed with Endia in his arms, speaking softly to her, and the Yellow crying and nodding, smiling intermittently.

"I understand," said the Red elf softly, making all in the room face her, Dalian with a mocking look of surprise. For once, she didn't need Aldrin to explain anything.

For a moment, no one said anything. The Guardian looked at them patiently, waiting for this moment to pass.

Dalian was the one to break the silence. "We need to keep moving. Are you all going to go in or are we skipping that?"

Zachtia looked at him thoughtfully. Should they all go in together? Would the mirrors show even more sad news?

"Let's see what we can together," said Aldrin, getting up, smoothing Endia's hair back and touching her cheek. "It might be less hard viewed as a group."

Endia nodded and followed him, and they all, in a line, walked back into the Mirror Room. When they arrived, Aldrin picked up and held Endia in his arms so all could stand together and watch.

The mirrors silently came to life again.

The far-left one showed all - including Aldrin - in gruesome fate, mangled and bleeding at the Purple's feet like Zachtia had seen before.

The center-left showed Endia and Zachtia walking into Zachtia's house with the figure in white waiting for them. "I didn't see this one," muttered Aldrin.

"What did you see?" asked Endia softly.

"You all crowded around me," the Green replied in a barely audible voice. "My face having a huge, fatal gash in it."

Endia shuddered and whimpered at the mental picture, curling her body into his.

Zachtia grasped Aldrin's arm. "Even if we have to carry you, Aldrin, we won't leave you," she said. "I promise."

Immediately, the images blurred and reshaped. All elves stared as the images repeated, but now Aldrin's body, either lying on the ground or supported by the two, was in the picture.

The center picture had Endia's body limply cradled onto Aldrin's with the Red elf rocking back and forth in anguish on her knees.

"Well that's something," exclaimed Aldrin in a hoarse whisper. "The very act of your promising to stay with me changed the outcome. I wonder…"

"Please indulge," said Zachtia, deciding to skip over the passionate carnal pleasure displayed on the center-right mirror, though her eye did catch in passing a Yellow elf on a chain in it now. "I'd really love some good news right about now."

"Well if it can be called good news," began Aldrin slowly. "You know how the elder scribe said that the mirrors were switched around at least twice in a day?"

"Yeah," nodded Endia, watching the last, least bloody future of Endia and Zachtia carrying Aldrin into Dairlo's house. "I thought it was some type of security measure."

"Exactly my thought," added Zachtia. She looked up at Aldrin. "What about it?"

"Wouldn't that mess with the reflection ever so slightly?" asked Aldrin urgently. "If the real mirror isn't placed in the exact place, wouldn't it produce a future that may be just slightly off?"

"Maybe…" Endia brightened, eyes wide. "You mean you might not be killed?"

"That's what I mean, and/or-" the Green gestured through the mirrors, "we might not all be killed, the figure in white may have already left, Zachtia won't make love to the Purple-"

"That's a false one," stated Zachtia flatly, frowning. "That's a Mica, that's a false one, no."

"And I might be just too injured to walk, not dead," finished Aldrin, gesturing towards the last mirror. "It's a hope and a chance we have to believe, but we have to prepare for any other outcome." He caught Zachtia's grimace and added, "Except that one.

They all walked out of the mirror room to find that the Guardian had died again. Now younger and more energetic again, he waved at them. "I hope everything goes wonderful," he said to them with a toothy grin. "I wouldn't want my new friends to be unduly treated by fate."

"Fate doesn't control us," Zachtia interjected firmly. "And we won't be pawns to it."

The Black elf of the group rose to his feet. Almost imperceptibly, he was shaking as he did so. He cracked his sardonic grin and said, "If all of you are satisfied," he said, a touch of impatience behind that wry smile, "We can be out of this place within the day."

He shook hands with the Guardian who gave him an appealing look. "Come back soon," the Goblyn said. "I know my older self wouldn't care if you do or don't, but I don't like being lonely. Alone, yes - love being alone, but never lonely." He looked with a curious frown at Dalian for a moment or two. "Well at least try to come back," he said under his breath. He then looked at the three other elves and said, "Goodbye, all! I hope you will all take what you've learned here and put it to good use."

"We will," said Aldrin softly, coming closer to the Goblyn. "And hopefully not just what we learned here in the Prophecy Room." He grasped the Guardian's hand. "Thank you for your hospitality."

"You're very welcome, my dear elf," said the Guardian softly. He turned to Zachtia. "May you teach your child well the history of the Goblyns, as well as your husband," he said. "And let them all know about the Guardian who let you sit in his chair."

Perhaps it was the wistfulness in his voice, or the weak chuckle he followed it up with, but Zachtia, to her own surprise, took up his hand in her two and grasped them tightly. "I will," she said solemnly. "And who knows? Maybe we'll return; come and visit you. We could even play a little Delie."

"I'd look forward to it!" replied the Goblyn brightly. "If your city is so close to here, we could probably have a picnic - goodbye Miss Yellow," he flipped over to Endia, who had by now gotten down from Aldrin's arms. He bent down and she grasped his hand. "May you have a wonderful life, my dear. You're very brave."

"Thank you," replied Endia with a small smile.

The elves looked back at the arched doorway they had crossed through onto the long bridge, looking at the Goblyn now a tiny speck in the brightly lit room. That is, at least what Zachtia observed.

"He's gone," whispered Aldrin, a touch of mourning in his voice. For once in this trip, he was in front of her, a mix of emotions and thoughts, and Zachtia could see his pursed lip expression return to his face. "I wonder if he's a figment in the past, or is truly eternal?"

"What do you mean, he's gone?" asked Zachtia, but instead of waiting for an answer, she caught up with Aldrin and looked back. As if time had one last trick to play, the light in the Prophecy Room was out, and there was no sign of the Guardian at its gates. "Oh, that's not fair," she groaned. "I thought we had gotten out of all of that time stuff."

"Remnants of the rift play out here, only subtly," replied their guide in front, and Zachtia looked around to him in surprise. His voice had been rather brusque. He seemed a little more hunched over, though just slightly.

"Are you alright, Dalian?"

Dalian straightened up, as if remembering he wasn't supposed to show anything out of the ordinary on this trip.

"I'm fine," he said, giving her that wry smile, though her senses - and perhaps motherly intuition - told her that it was fake. "We just need to keep moving."

Aldrin came up beside him and touched his arm. "Dalian, we're all companions here," he said softly. "We know you're not okay."

"Then let's get moving so I'll *be* okay," Dalian snapped. He gestured out towards the long bridge. "Shall we? Come on."

Aldrin and Zachtia, and then Aldrin and Endia all exchanged worried looks at each other, and followed, Aldrin once again taking the lead behind Dalian, Endia in-between, and Zachtia following up the rear. The Red approved of this to her own surprise, as, if Dalian were to suddenly snap or turn on them, Aldrin would be there to deal with him. She had caught the thought as it passed off the top of Aldrin's mind and she was grateful.

Dalian led them across the long, stone bridge. All three of the elves new to this part of the cave were on edge; if Dalian was on edge, maybe there were traps that he hadn't told them about. But why would he lead them out just for them to succumb to a Goblyn trap? Didn't they all trust him?

They did… but all of them now could see a slight tremor in his hands and the way he stalked more than walked in front of them.

Finally, they reached the other side of the cave that was the Goblyn City. They saw the Lumen that connected via the branches of light throughout the city glowing dismally like a fire burned through the night.

"Tread carefully here," came Dalian's voice in front of them, and Zachtia looked down. In front of them began the insidious littering of Onyx and Mica stones like way back when in the entrance of the cave in Wanderer's Bane. They might still be in Wanderer's Bane, she mused, or just the end of it. She then realized that she could see the ground more clearly now due to a light source above them. It was unrefined Lumen sticking out of the ceiling, shining their light collected from whatever light was ahead, shining into the end of the tunnel. She wanted to run with excitement, they were almost there, almost out of the Goblyn Mines!

They reached halfway through the tunnel and Dalian stopped in front of them, swaying unsteadily. "This is where I leave you," he said with a small grin. "We must do this again sometime."

"Dalian, why don't you come with us?" asked Aldrin with urgency. "We can all see you're not well, you can stay in Scarlesh and gather your strength."

"It's not that kind of illness, don't you get it?" barked their guide with sudden fury. "I can't just eat and sleep it off, I have to go back - and I will make it, I can tell you that." He gave a ghastly version of that wry smile as he turned to Aldrin. "The mirror on the far right, right?"

Aldrin blinked and then nodded slowly. "That was my guess. I hoped it was."

"It is," said Dalian urgently. "And do you know what it showed me, Aldrin? It showed me when I was going to die, and I don't die here, okay?" His voice was becoming higher with strain and he started walking past Aldrin, "So let's leave on good terms."

He knocked into Aldrin and lost his balance. Aldrin tried to catch him but the Black Elf stumbled backwards, his feet dug into the floor frantically - and loosened one of the stones.

Both Endia and Zachtia were suddenly pinned to the wall by Aldrin as the ceiling rumbled above Dalian and a split second later rocks and Lumen shards of the ceiling came crashing down around the Black elf.

For a moment, all stood still.

Zachtia didn't know for a moment whether the entire tunnel would collapse on them or just that section. After a moment, with the ceiling remaining intact, save a few stones from that area littering down, all the elves neared their fallen comrade.

Endia had her hand to her chest. "Oh no," she whispered faintly.

Dalian was lying under the pile of rubble. A wet redness was seeping through his clothing and blood trickled out of his mouth. His eyes seemed to focus on Aldrin and he choked out in utter bewilderment, "This... this isn't right."

Then his eyes glazed over. His body relaxed to move no longer.

Aldrin knelt down beside the body of the Black Elf and Zachtia heard him say some sort of final rites as he closed the darkened eyes of the body. He lowered his head and took a deep breath.

"Aldrin," offered Zachtia, not daring to move for fear of flipping more stones, "you were too far away to help him. You kept us safe."

"I know," whispered Aldrin. "But it doesn't make it any easier." With another heavy sigh, he got up and carefully walked over to her and Endia. He picked up Endia and cradled her close to his body, and Zachtia could see wetness on his cheeks.

After a moment, he said, "Come on. We're so close." With an effort, he turned away from the body and made careful steps towards the stone stairway that had been their goal for the past few days.

Zachtia followed. She wanted to give him some comforting words or even a hug, but both of them were too focused on keeping their steps. Soon though, they came to where the tunnel evened out - no Mica or Onyx to jostle, and the steps were before them like old friends greeting them after a long journey.

Chapter 17

Aldrin put Endia down and gestured for Zachtia to go in front of him, which she did with a grateful smile and a nod. Up the stairs they climbed and the area seemed to get brighter and brighter. This pure, natural light seemed so foreign to them and they blinked up at it. It was like walking the stairway into a new world.

Finally, after what seemed like hours of climbing - and in reality, it had only been a few minutes - they broke out into a brilliant, blinding light, and reached ground that felt soft and grassy soon after.

They had made it.

But they had two more obstacles, Zachtia knew. One was Shield Forest, the dense forest that was a natural guarding wall of Scarlesh, and the second was their pursuer: the Purple that she could just sense faintly in the back of her mind. He was only an hour, maybe less away from the group.

For a moment, they all just stood there, drinking in the sunlight's warm, nourishing rays. A few times they had all wondered if winter had come while they were in the Mines, but no, the grass was still green and the evening sun still shined bright and graciously upon the three elves.

They also had to stand there for a while, blinking. All the while they were in the mines, they had to consciously brighten their elven vision against the darkness of the caves and even in the places of the Tower where it had grown dim. Now in natural sunlight, they had to almost forcibly reel those senses back in.

Finally, a small but mature voice came from her lower left. "I can't believe he's dead." Zachtia looked down at Endia, or at least tried to as her vision was still blurry in the sunlight. She could make out the young woman was crying. But not like a child's cry. Her voice was that of an adult's at a funeral pier. "He was so close."

"And yet so far," replied Aldrin. Zachtia glared at him through her eyelids but his own eyes were closed as he continued, "He would have to have made that entire journey in reverse. If he tripped over a stone, then he would have had dozens more opportunities to…" He sighed. "But, his death actually gives me hope."

"In what way?" asked the Red. She could see a blurry visage of him now.

"He said that he wouldn't die at that time, he thought he would make it," said Endia, looking up at her. Aldrin nodded as she continued, "Therefore when he died… he proved that even the 'right' mirror, the 'right' outcome could still be wrong."

"Unless of course we all chose the wrong mirror," muttered Zachtia. She could see better now. The ground they were standing on steepled up from the ground below on all sides, camouflaging the entrance to the Mines as ground. She could see Shield Forest, and beyond she knew would be her home. "We should get moving," she said. A pang of warning had shoved itself against the pang of wistful hope. "That Purple will be here soon."

"Do you think we'll get to Scarlesh before he gets to us?" asked Endia anxiously.

Aldrin was silent for a moment and Zachtia knew he was crunching his numbers. "… no." he said finally. "Once he comes out of the Wanderer's Bane, he'll make a beeline for us. We will have to face him."

Endia must have been thinking about the same mirror outcomes that Zachtia was for she shuddered and Zachtia could see she was trying not to panic.

"That means," the Red of the group said, "that I need to make up a strategy to do so." She looked at Aldrin and held up a finger to stave off whatever surprised comment he had. "You've done so much for me this trip," she said. "And if it weren't for the actions of Dalian, you probably would've done a lot more. But I am a Red Elf, wife of Dairlo. Let me play my part."

The Green's jaw snapped shut and he nodded. "Let's walk while you're thinking," he said.

So they walked, and Zachtia thought. She thought a great deal, having many scenarios in her head and slowly crossing them out one-by-one, eliminating the impossible and the improbable. "Aldrin," she asked softly and the Green looked at her, "How do you go about displacing things?"

The Green blinked. "I've never been asked to describe it before."

"You said it was some type of concentration," urged Zachtia. "And that you have a bag full of stuff around your shoulder like your cape and such."

"My cape, my hat, my buffalo arrows, yes. Hm." He pursed his lips while thinking. "As for the concentration, I'd guess I'd describe it as converting that want for the tool as a need."

"I don't understand," Zachtia said after a while.

"Well, think of it like you need your husband. You don't just want him, you need him. If he were displaced in front of you, I think even you could bring him out of displacement with that need if you concentrated hard enough. Otherwise it'd take both you and Endia..." He paused thoughtfully but then furthered "Like a child's 'need' for a toy, or an enemy's 'need' for revenge. It's not a 'need' but a want, but that want is so strong that — Creator save us..."

He stopped abruptly both in speech and in walk, his eyes wide and heartbeat suddenly akimbo. His thoughts were suddenly hyper-focused in his shock and realization and Zachtia and Endia stopped and looked at him with surprise and worry. "What is it?" asked Endia as Zachtia asked "What's wrong?"

When he spoke, the Green elf's voice was in a whisper and his eyes, still as wide as tent-peg tops, were locked on Zachtia. "It's not you he's after. It's me."

Endia gasped and her "Oh!" came out throttled.

Zachtia was dumbfounded as well. "He's after you?" she asked. "Why do you think so?"

Aldrin's hands were up in an almost pleading gesture. "It's for revenge," he said, voice still soft. "I killed his mate with my arrow, or at least injured her. Now he wants revenge. He wouldn't pursue you all the way just to eat you or, Creator forbid, mate with you. He would come after — is coming after me."

That certainly switched up a few of Zachtia's strategies. All this time, half of them involved her being the bait, the deer in front of the tripwire. Now with Aldrin being the one wanted...

They were passing into the forest now. Zachtia didn't know the forest entirely offhand, but she did know of a few places that would be the ideal setup for a trap. She was glad at least this time, in this forest, it wasn't raining. "Alright, follow me," she said to Aldrin and Endia, and picked up the pace.

There were five bows forming a pentagon in the trees. They weren't even proper bows, save the center one. All the others were strong branches hurriedly tested and fitted with bowstrings. But they would work.

Aldrin fitted the last buffalo arrow into the last bow. He worked with frantic but careful speed. Careful not to dislodge any of the branches so precariously pulling the strings of the bows, all connected by one long rope.

Endia was already in her hiding place, while Zachtia was in front of him, slowly playing out the rope.

The Purple was nearly to the forest. It was gaining speed, like Aldrin had foretold.

"I hope this works," the Red elf said through gritted teeth. She gave Aldrin her most hopeful smile. "Far right mirror," she stated.

"Far right mirror," repeated Aldrin, not looking but gleaning from her sense what she was doing. "Thank you, Zachtia. It will work," he added firmly.

Now the trap was set. The bait walked solemnly to his designated spot, saying a silent prayer. He may be so sure with Zachtia that the trap would work. He wished he was as confident about it himself. It was very makeshift, and they dare not test it with the allotted time they had. Within five minutes, maybe less, that Purple was going to storm through that clearing and if everything went well, he would be crowned with an array of five arrows through the skull.

That thundercloud feeling was back as he got into position, his entire body in a crouch of concentrated energy. His hunting knife was in his hand, ready to come up and out into the weak spots of any mortal beings.

Five minutes.

He stood there patiently, his focus on the entranceway that the Purple was most likely to take. Sure enough, the dusty, fear-shaped thundercloud of feeling was coming from that direction. He slowed his breathing, forcing himself to relax.

Four minutes.

Something tugged at his mind. It was like a grapple had been thrown into his mind but had only skidded and had not caught on anything. He kept himself focused, though in this state he could feel everything around him: the stilted air that seemed to whisper at him through the trees, the patchy ground beneath his feet, even the surface thoughts and feelings of Zachtia and Endia.

Three minutes.

There. On the near horizon, that shape, that mental-visual storm was taking shape, coming out of the forest before the Purple would like a dense fog. He immediately masked his mind again, getting the weird feeling of deja vu. The feelings of welcome and of happiness had shielded the minds of the Reds from the fog, but now that it was coming for him and him alone…

He felt the grapple flung into his mind skid again, missing its target. He concentrated further on both keeping himself invisible from the other mind or nearly invisible, as well as keeping in the zeroed in-focused position of the hunter. This would be a quick battle.

Two minutes.

The Purple stopped.

Aldrin could sense the actual bodily sense of the Purple stop in its tracks. That inglorious hunter wasn't coming any nearer, as if it sensed something was up. The mind fog around Aldrin's feet, not affecting him because of his cloaked mind, twisted and jerked like a sea of confusion. Then it settled, becoming like tentacles of mist as, to the Green's horror, the Purple started stalking a wide circle *around* the trap.

He looked at Zachtia and saw her wide eyes, she had sensed it too. He felt her sense drop from his mind and knew she was cloaking herself as well. For a brief moment, he felt what was like a glimmer of thought in her direction – the child in her womb – before that was masked as well.

He hadn't sensed Endia at all ever since she had hidden behind her tree. That was the power of the Yellow Elves.

His internal timer halted on two minutes, Aldrin let his mind feel the Purple walk around in a wide, hesitant circle. Many a time he had held his breath as the Purple had walked towards Zachtia's hiding spot, but then decided against it.

Now he was coming around to where he was directly behind Aldrin, and the Green set his teeth, turned around in his crouched position, and uncloaked his mind. The trap was set.

The brain fog attacked him. It slammed into him like an attacking drake and he felt all of his senses go berserk. Pangs of fear like those felt in the Cafeterium or the Throne Room tore at his heart like knives, but he fought back, thinking of all things wonderful. Thinking of home. Thinking of the encounters and blessings he had had over the past month. He thought about Endia.

And that was when the Purple came galloping through the dense underbrush like a tiger, snarling and opening its maw.

Or at least, that is when Aldrin perceived him coming. Even when his dagger in hand came up to slash at the Purple's throat, he felt the claws of the massive beastly elf dig into his shoulders. He twisted and drove both of his fist and the dagger into where the Purple's head would be, barely saving himself from the beast's teeth being sunk into his throat.

He was fighting under something worse than blindness: slow motion. Every move Aldrin perceived was coming at milliseconds to seconds too late! With an effort, he kicked the beast hard in the stomach and watched it as it seemingly took its time to topple over in the opposite direction he was falling, of which the sight was a soft slowness but he felt the ground hit hard and fast.

Aldrin got up just in time to see the creature get up and he watched as it came at him. He jumped back but felt its claws slash through the top layers of his tunic and skin. He tried for one cold-cocked blow and felt his fist connect with the Purple's nose before he saw it happen. He wondered for a split second whether to just close his eyes and go by the other senses the Purple's mind wasn't attacking, but he realized that the Purple and he had circled to where the Purple was near the correct spot for the trap!

Sure enough, when the attack came and he fell backwards onto his back, he heard the *Schlick!* of arrows being loosed and finding their way into a body. However, when the image came to his slow-seeing eyes, it revealed that although all arrows had been loosed, only three had found their way into the Purple, only one of them going into his skull through his eye socket. The others buried themselves into his arms and he yowled such a cry it paralyzed Aldrin for a split second.

Aldrin felt the body of the Purple come upon him and his face suddenly felt hot and wet as the claws of the cursed elf raked up his face from his nose to his ear! How badly, he couldn't tell. Blindly and with a blunt prayer, Aldrin whisked up his knife in both hands with all his strength.

Before his vision started swimming, he saw that his knife had gone up, plunged into the base of the Purple's neck, and tore all the way up until it was now buried hilt deep in the creature's jaw.

Zachtia watched as the two-minute battle came to an end and ran over to Aldrin's side. Endia was there as well, and together they rolled the still oozing body off of Aldrin's own.

He was shaking, his eyes were closed and his face was one massive mess of red and black blood. "That went well," he choked out, coughing on the liquid that had found its way into his mouth. "Need to fix... need to dress." He groaned and the arms that were spasmodically reaching around his body now fell limply to the ground.

"How do we fix this?" asked Zachtia, trying very hard to keep the rising fear out of her voice. "Do you have — you have a medicinal kit, don't you?" she asked, fearing the answer.

There was no answer, just a heavy breath, followed by another.

She set her jaw and looked at a wide-eyed Endia. "Come on," she said firmly. "I'll need your help."

Endia nodded and came around to Zachtia's side, the side of Aldrin that had his displaced bag. Zachtia put her hand on Endia's outstretched one and then, thinking it would help, closed her eyes. She thought hard. This bag, they needed this bag. They needed the medicinal kit.

For a while, nothing happened, and she felt Endia starting to panic as Aldrin started to groan.

Aldrin.

"We need Aldrin alive," she barked to Endia, snapping her focus back to the matter at hand. "We need him alive, so we need that kit – and we need that bag – agh!"

Suddenly it felt as if she had stuck her hand into an ant mound or a beehive, and by Endia's cry she knew she felt it too. But they also felt something else. Material, the material of a bag like a burlap sack.

Hands still curled together, they numbly felt up the bag until they found its opening, and then spent the next five minutes in concentrated agony as they fished around in the bag for a sack or a box.

Zachtia felt something definite, hoped it was the right item and she pulled hers and Endia's hands along with the object out of the bag. Soon, the stinging buzzing abruptly stopped and they both opened their eyes.

Held in their hands was a box. It was heavier than it was when it had been displaced. It had the designs of the Medicinal Ward, to their great relief. Zachtia opened it frantically and found to her further relief a bottle of the Gardener's Salve. She could hardly believe it. This salve was so precious and so powerful that, for a second, she just looked at the clear, bluish liquid. Then, shaking herself, she uncorked the bottle and gingerly poured some into each heavy gash in Aldrin's face.

Aldrin gasped as the liquid looked as if it were eating away at the gash… and then his breaths became more regular and more peaceful. "Pineapple," he muttered bewilderingly, and he fell asleep as the lady elves cried and breathed huge sighs of relief.

A Warrior's Code

It was three days that they stayed in the forest, not daring to move Aldrin. Zachtia carefully reapplied the healing salve at the appropriate times and soon the injuries, though still there, were no longer life-threatening.

The two women had lugged the guts of the Purple far enough away that the smell wasn't as pungent. They hadn't been able to clean themselves or Aldrin yet, and so smelled of grime, sweat, and old blood.

After lugging the Purple away, Endia never left Aldrin's side. Zachtia was surprised that there were no guards or spies in the forest, someone had definitely slackened security at Scarlesh. Well, she would at least have scouts keeping watch. She was sure her husband would too.

Finally, on the third day at mid-morning, Aldrin opened his eyes. He had opened them before, but only briefly, but now he opened them and looked around. He sat up and Endia knelt beside him and hugged his side to help him keep his balance.

"Hello," he said to her with a small smile. His jaw slackened a bit but then his smile broadened as he saw the medicinal kit on the ground, its salve bottle nearly empty, and he looked up at Zachtia. "You ladies did't," he said, his voice hoarse, coming out of a dry throat. "'m very proud of you."

Endia hugged him for real this time.

"Take me to my husband."

The words were hard and cold and the guards at the threshold of Scarlesh blinked in surprise. They immediately recognized Zachtia, wife and consort of Dairlo, a recently retired Captain. But to see her as if she had come from a long battle, smelling of grime and grit and with an arm helping to support an elf in green clothing gave them pause.

"Now, please," she said firmly. "We have come a long way to find him. Take us to my husband." She glared at the righthand guard who was about to keep Aldrin at bay and added threateningly "All of us."

The guards looked at each other, shrugged, and turned to the large, thick gate of the large, thick wall surrounding the city. The left one unlocked the set of smaller doors within the gate and they all entered, the guards only now seeing a third of the party, dressed in yellow, scurrying up behind Zachtia and the Green.

Finally. After what seemed like months of walking, climbing, fighting, crying, watching people die, almost getting killed themselves, Aldrin, Endia, and Zachtia all crossed the threshold into Scarlesh. They were not the same band of companions as when they had met. For one thing, they were a party of three instead of two; a trio that had grown under pressure in friendship.

For another thing, it wasn't the Green supporting the Red anymore. The residents of Scarlesh watched with astonishment and apprehension a little woman dressed in yellow came up beside the stumbling but determined Green and both she and Zachtia gently helped him keep upright as they walked down the Main Street of Scarlesh. They were also flanked by two guards with bemused expressions.

All within the group were filthy and smelled of unwashed body dirt, and in the Green's case, dried blood.

Zachtia knew what they were thinking. It was scandalous, helping a Green. She didn't care. The war was over, the Reds had won, but at what a cost. How had hate trickled down from the Council and snowballed into all-out war? The more she thought about it, the more set in her determination she was.

She was also looking for her husband. She didn't know where he was, but she could sense him even as they had drawn near the city from the forest. His sense truly gave coming into Scarlesh the sense of coming home. It was almost as strong as what the Black Elves must have felt in Wanderer's Bane.

The two guards stopped in front of two more guards and stopped the group. "The wife of Captain Dairlo'Ecduv'Demallahush wishes to see her husband," the one on the left said.

"She may, she is expected," replied the opposite guard on the left. He looked at Aldrin and Endia sharply. "But those accompanying her will have to be taken into custody. It is not lawful for a Gree-"

"These two are with me," stated Zachtia firmly. "Both have sacrificed nearly everything so that I could arrive here, in Scarlesh, to be with my husband. We have traveled many miles together," she furthered, her voice becoming the voice she would use to talk to her husband's troops. "We have supped and starved together. These are my kin. My brother and my sister – regardless of their color!" She heard the murmuring of the crowd. "Let us all pass to my husband," she ordered the guards.

For a long moment, the guards did nothing. Zachtia watched tensely as the crowd started murmuring louder. "Poor woman's deranged," she heard repeated in variety through the crowd.

The guards must have heard it too. "Maybe you should all come with us," said the one on the right, not without apprehension, looking into the lady's furious eyes. "Maybe after we get your interrogation through-"

An overruling, commanding and very much missed voice called out from behind them, "You will do no such thing!"

It was all Zachtia could do to keep herself from crying as all turned and saw Captain Dairlo'Ecduv'Demallahush walking purposefully towards the group, his jaw set, and something glinting in his right hand. "I bear the seal of the Council of Four," he called out. He brandished the circlet that bore the symbol of the Council City and the Four Towers Library. "I command all of you to stand down. Let all pass and be welcomed." He looked at his wife and his look softened to a quiet smile. "For they are the saviors of and apparently kin to my wife – and therefore to me!"

All the guards took four steps back in perfect unison and Aldrin looked at Dairlo unsteadily. "Thank you," the Green whispered, and the little Yellow beside him nodded eagerly.

In a gesture that surprised even Zachtia, Dairlo gently moved Endia aside and took up her spot. "Do you need help getting the rest of the way?" he asked Aldrin, who was starting to sway forward rather dangerously.

"I think I can manage," said the Green with a smile, and then collapsed.

Aldrin awoke to the feeling of a cloth dabbing his face. He was lying on his back and he looked up.

Endia's face beamed down at him and she dipped the small cloth back into water, rung it out, and applied it again very gently to his face. "How are you, Aldrin?" she asked softly.

"Alive," he said, sighing with sudden relief at the monumental statement. "And awake… and feeling very gross, but if that's the worst problem I have then I'm very grateful."

She chuckled and dabbed some more with the cloth. "Captain Dairlo said that as soon as you were steady on your feet you could use their bath," she said, giving careful attention to his ears with the wet cloth.

"I'll thank him when I see him," replied Aldrin, looking around himself. He wasn't on a bed, but instead a cushioned shelf beside a large stain-glass window. Bookshelves were on either side of him, and his legs had had to be bent slightly and tilted against the wall to fit him on the shelf.

Dairlo's house was all one floor and almost all one room, with a kitchen and dining table all in one area, a living room where Aldrin was, and presumably behind the large drape that covered a large bit of the corner of the room, was Dairlo and Zachtia's bed. Aldrin figured that the bath was outside, or in an enclosed booth attached to the house.

"How about you?" he asked Endia, reaching up and taking her hand gently in his. "How are you, Endia?"

"I'm well," started the Yellow. Her eyes glistened as she added, "I'm so relieved. The, uh, mirror on the far right was closest, by the way. But it was Dairlo and two of the guards that carried you in."

"Hm." He didn't let go of her hand. "Relieved," he repeated.

"Yes, relieved," furthered Endia. "Relieved we weren't killed, relieved that Dairlo is so nice and..." She looked at her hand in his. "And you're still alive," she said. "I don't know what I'd do if you had..." She gently stroked his hand with her other hand. "Aldrin, I know that you're still faithful to your mate who died... and I understand that. But, I also want you to know that you're loved." A tear fell down her cheek. "Loved so dearly. She was so blessed – they were so blessed to have you as a father and husband."

He looked up at her. "Endia," he said finally. "What you say is true. I will forever keep Malendire, Fennec, and Mayberry in my mind. In my soul. But let me tell you this..." He put her knuckles to his lips and felt his own eyes tear up. "One thing they never wanted me to be was alone and depressed. Malendire wouldn't want that. If this blossoms into something more... I wouldn't reject it."

Endia, tears now streaming down her face, licked her lips, bent down, and then kissed Aldrin's forehead. "I wouldn't either," she whispered.

Dairlo's whole postural attitude was one of deep attention and thought; his eyes, slightly closed, looked gently but intensely at his wife, his back hunched so his arms sat near his kneecaps, hands pressed together with fingers steepled.

Zachtia knew he was listening. She also knew he wanted to be touching her, feeling that warmth that had been displaced from him for almost a month now. But now wasn't the time for touching, she knew. There was a time and place for everything, and touching in a warm, tearful embrace and a deep, soul-felt kiss had come as soon as the guards were away and the door was closed. That was in its time, and now the time had come for her to give her account.

So she did. She told him everything, from that rainy night when she threw rocks at Aldrin, to the prison, right up to when they came into the city. Dairlo only interrupted her for simple questions, of which he had few. She knew she was giving more information than a Red usually would, but she wanted to tell him everything, and there was a *lot* of everything.

Finally, she stopped. She had been holding a glass of water in her hands while she had been talking and had been taking sips from it. It felt like one of the best feelings of the world, the cool water running across her tongue and down her throat, which had been parched many times during the journey.

She had changed too, into a relaxed evening dress. The fabric felt like lilac petals across her skin rather than the metal-laced satin she wore while in the field.

She drained what was left in her cup and let out a sigh, looking at her husband who hadn't moved in position for the past half hour as he now got up and stretched his back.

"Thank you," he said softly. "You've made everything very clear." He walked over to the table and brought back the pitcher of water. "Very clear," he repeated, refilling her cup. "I'll send word to Fyreton to warn them about Wanderer's Bane and its inhabitants. And I will tell my men to find and bury the body of the Purple. No need for that smell to attract other Purples."

He poured his own cup of water and set the pitcher back down on the table. "Eighteen men," he said softly. "Three women, one child. The drakes turned the tide, did their job. But at what cost."

He sat down in front of Zachtia and both were silent for a moment.

"I haven't asked yet," said Zachtia, brushing her hand against his knee, "How goes the war?"

He grunted and remained silent for a few seconds, staring into his water. "What war?" he asked finally, his voice anything but joyful or victorious. "We won."

His previous words repeated in Zachtia's mind.

But at what cost.

Epilogue

Aldrin and Endia spent a week at Dairlo's house. It wasn't as awkward as Aldrin thought it would be. Many times during this trip, he wondered how he would go about dropping off Zachtia at Scarlesh. There was the possibility he considered before they even entered the Yellow Encampment that he would simply wave goodbye to her as he stood at the outskirts of Barrier Forest, watching her enter Scarlesh on her own. There was also the possibility of him following her into Scarlesh and beating a hasty retreat, or else end up as a prisoner of war.

But when the actual time came, he found that he was treated as a guest. Dairlo'Ecduv'Demallahush was one of the most civil – if not one of the quietest — hosts he had ever been in the home of. When he was well, he slept on a camping cot next to the window, Endia having a similar cot in the corner. Meals were eaten regularly, and during those times, the Red even attempted more than just the daily reports, helped along by Zachtia, who had had some more practice in the matter.

Aldrin eventually remembered what Aleborne asked him to tell Dairlo, and the Red had stared at him in a reverent sort of sadness. Dairlo had then, to his wife's astonishment, asked Aldrin to go into detail on what happened in Fyreton and what had happened to the warden.

Aldrin had come to respect Dairlo and had forgiven him for what he had to do in the war; Dairlo had been the first to compliment him on a certain battle during the war, but out of respect hadn't asked him how they had managed the tactically genius strategy.

The Red had then apologized for what happened to Aldrin's city and his family. After a pause and a deep sigh, Aldrin responded simply, "It wasn't *your* idea. But thank you."

By the end of the week, Aldrin knew it was time to go. He had healed, save the scars on his shoulders, chest, and face, but those would disappear over time. Almost sadly, Aldrin and Endia walked out of Scarlesh with the eyes of everyone on them. Everyone, but most importantly Zachtia and Dairlo, with the hope for a better way of life in Zachtia's womb.

"So, where to now?" asked Endia, looking up at Aldrin at the precipice of the Satin Trails, courtesy of Dairlo's instructions. "Are we going to go back home?"

"Back to the Yellow forest?" asked Aldrin. He had frowned a little and then nodded in understanding. "If you want to, yes. I have something to do before I decide what I'm going to do after it."

"I don't need to go there immediately," said Endia quickly, not wanting him to think she was trying to desert him. "Though father would be very glad to see me. What do you need to do?"

After a pause to form the words, Aldrin said finally, "I need to go back to what's left of Emeretl — my city, the one that was destroyed by the Red vengeance attack. That is a spot that is burning a hole in my heart and I can't go through life thinking about it so vehemently."

"What are you going to do?" asked Endia quietly, taking his hand in hers and giving it a squeeze.

"Take what's left of my house and burn it," said Aldrin, his voice quivering. "Burn it to ashes. To make the ghosts of my past stop haunting my future." He sighed, as if resettling a heavy weight upon his shoulders. "To let go."

He looked down at Endia and found her beaming at him. Those beautiful eyes proud and glistening in empathy for him.

"I'll come with you," she said. "If you'll have me."

Aldrin grinned, and squeezed her hand. "I would like nothing better."

It took a week to get to the territory of Emeretl, allowing Aldrin and Endia to talk intimately with each other. Aldrin talked about his past, letting it pour out of him, as if bringing to mind all the things he was going to watch burn and fade.

Endia talked about her past life too, giving cheerful memories and wistful memories. Part of her didn't want to return, for fear she would be sucked back into that life, courtesy of her cowardly father. The other part missed him very dearly. Aldrin promised the next stop after Emeretl would be the Yellow Village, and also that he would stay there for as long as she liked.

They crept up upon the hill that overlooked the small city and Aldrin steadied himself for this return. He *had* to do this. For him. For his future. … maybe even for Endia.

They came up to where they were standing on the hill, and there, in the near center of the town before them, stood a figure dressed in white, its garb covering its entire body, with a hood over its head and a sash covering its mouth.

When they drew nearer, the figure removed the sash and lifted the hood, showing the figure to be the one that had given

A Warrior's Code

Dairlo instructions at Fyreton, and who had known where she was going to finally meet the weary travelers.

"Gardener," said Aldrin.

There was no surprise in his voice. There almost wasn't even any reverence like Dalian had intoned. In fact, there was a very slight undertone of annoyance, as if greeting a guest late to the party.

Endia looked up at the Green and then at Gardener in surprise. "Is it really her?" she asked, her reverent tone more than enough to share between her and Aldrin.

"Yes, it's me, my young Yellow," said the young, ancient lady with a smile. Her tone then turned serious. "Aldrin. I know you've come from a long journey. I'm very proud of you for it, for the warrior's code you upheld in your travels and with Zachtia and Dairlo."

"Thank you," returned Aldrin simply.

"And now I sense you have come to bury the dead," she continued. "Or at least the ghosts of the dead. I respect that and approve."

Aldrin, for the moment, was feeling particularly Red at the moment. Maybe being with Zachtia had rubbed off on *him* as well. "Excuse me, Gardener, but I can't help but feel that you're leading up to something. Please come to it."

Gardener looked at him, and then, in a slightly guilty tone replied,

"You are right. We — meaning those who occupy the Council Towers and the Four Towers Library, need your help."

Made in the USA
Middletown, DE
11 February 2020